I0835476

DARK MATCH

Dark Match

J.L. Minyard

This book is a work of fiction. Names, characters, places, and incidents are either products of the author's imagination or are used fictitiously. Any semblance to actual persons, living or dead, events, or locales is entirely coincidental.

hello@jessicaminyard.com

Cover by Cormar Covers

Interior graphics by mgsdesiigns / eBook map design by Books and Moods

Editing by Erica Edits

http://www.ericaedits.com/

ISBN: 978-1-957004-19-8

eBook ISBN: 978-1-957004-18-1

20260302

Content Notes

This book contains material that may be sensitive to some readers.

CWs: explicit sex and language, brief alcohol use, discussions of money, past money troubles, pegging, a description of menstruation.

Chapter One
Raleigh

Raleigh was supposed to be balls-deep in dick right now, but instead she was bleeding into the man's toilet.

New Year's Eve was going perfectly. She and Harper rolled into the bar in skimpy, spangled dresses—Harper almost flashed everyone dancing—and Raleigh hadn't paid for a drink all night. At the end of the night, Harper would go home to Jesse Lee, and Raleigh would go home with whomever she wanted.

She'd decided on Ben Ramirez early. He was a spark plug of a man, short and stocky, with a square jaw and curly man bun. Yes, he was one of Teddy's wrestlers, and she had a rule about fucking where she worked, but options were limited when you went to the only bar in town. Ben also had the kind of rakish reputation that she liked: no strings attached.

The free tequila shots blunted the tell-tale cramps until it was almost too late.

They weren't being dulled now; pain radiated through her lower back and down her thighs as she hunched over Ben's toilet.

Her period had always been an obnoxious, unpredictable nuisance. She'd go months without it and then it would arrive with a painful vengeance. She could bleed and spot anywhere from three days to a couple weeks. Birth control was hit or miss, and she was currently in between prescriptions because the last pill made her bloated and angry.

She usually carried an emergency stash of everything—tampons in various sizes, pads, panty liners, Midol. But the clutch that matched her dress was tiny. She had taken a calculated risk.

Now, instead of having sex with Ben Ramirez, she was trapped in his bathroom and pondering how to extricate herself.

Ben's bathroom wasn't the nastiest man's bathroom she had ever seen, but it wasn't well stocked, either. The roll of toilet paper was almost done, and she couldn't even see a hand towel. She wasn't above stealing a hand towel if it allowed her to leave with some shred of her dignity left.

She thumbed through her text messages with Harper.

RIP

I'll just die here, I guess

Omg

Do you want me to come get you??

Raleigh sucked in a breath as another cramp decimated her uterus. Harper's offer was tempting. Would she come alone, or bring Jesse Lee, Ben's coach, with her? How much of a shit show would that be?

There was a knock on the door.

Oh, no.

Hold that thought.

"Raleigh?"

The voice on the other side definitely did not belong to Ben.

Raleigh frowned, her pulse kicking up a notch. "August?"

What the fuck was August doing here?

August Callahan was another of Teddy's wrestlers and bartended at End O' Road, but she didn't remember seeing him there tonight.

Jesse had turned August into some kind of wrestling protégé. He had been booking bigger and bigger shows recently, and was slated to make his TV debut with the

Kentucky and Indiana Grappling Underground promotion in two weeks. The pressure was driving Teddy up a wall, which in turn drove Raleigh up the wall right along with him as his executive assistant. Teddy was bound and determined to have August snatched up as his first big star.

She had been pulling long hours, doing work she was in no way qualified to do, and she felt she deserved a night of drunken debauchery.

"Yeah, hey, it's me." His voice pitched higher, as if pleased she'd recognized him by sound alone.

August was a sweet kid, clean cut and polite, which was totally not her type. She liked them a little rougher. She knew August was harboring some kind of unrequited crush. He'd blush and look at his toes whenever she spoke to him, and she'd caught him tracking her movements through the gym more than once.

Plus, she had her "no fucks at work" policy.

Raleigh sighed, propping her chin on her palm. Her ass was going numb from sitting so long.

"Yeah, hi, hello. Can I help you?"

"Are you...okay?"

She stared forlornly at the tiny black thong stretched between her legs, nowhere large enough to accommodate a pad. "Not really."

There was a pause, but Raleigh didn't hear any footsteps move away from the door. To be fair, she hadn't heard him approach, either, but she had been preoccupied with her current predicament.

"Can I...help? I mean, what can I do to help? I'm available to help, I mean. Ben's kind of passed out on the couch."

Ah. Well, that would explain why she had been able to hide out for so long.

"Uh, what are you doing here?"

"Oh." Another pause. "Uh, I live here."

Oh, roommates. August was Ben's roommate. She couldn't begrudge anyone having a roommate, not in this economy. It's not like any of them could afford mortgages, even in their tiny town.

Raleigh was lucky. Teddy Myles paid her good money, especially for a girl like her. It was more than she—a backwoods hick with a high school diploma and no college—could hope for. She was supposed to have been barefoot and pregnant before eighteen, like the majority of the French women, but had somehow escaped that fate.

Not by her own choice, though. Her high school boyfriend, whose parents owned the local grocery store, didn't want that life. He wanted college and law school and big cities and bright lights. So, he left.

Her mother was always salty about that. About Raleigh losing out on such a catch of a man. Teddy Myles was her unicorn.

She had no idea what she wanted to do with her life, anyway. It was hard to have dreams and aspirations when you never had any dreams or aspirations.

She was originally only supposed to be the cute girl at the front desk—her ass looked great in spandex. But then she turned out to be competent at so many unexpected things. And she didn't take any shit from wrestlers and gym bros.

"Well." She wiggled a bit on the toilet to try to restore feeling back in her legs. "I'm in the middle of a feminine emergency and I don't have any feminine products." Might as well be honest about it and see if August was still willing to rescue her. "And I'd really like to take a shower since I bled all over my legs."

More silence.

This was the part where August fled for his life.

"Can I come in?"

That...was not what she was expecting. Her thong was around her ankles. She tried to pull her tight dress down as far as it would go so she wouldn't accidentally expose any parts.

"Yeah, okay. Enter at your own risk." She snickered.

The bathroom door swung open and in stepped August Callahan, as brave as could be.

Oh, no.

He was wearing gray sweats.

And *only* gray sweats, the waistband slung low on his hips. August may have been sweeter than homemade sweet tea, but the boy was also hot as fuck.

Most of the wrestlers shaved their chests, and his was smooth. There wasn't a hair in sight on his sculpted pecs, or the space under his belly button, or in the cuts of his hips. What hair he did have—on his head, over his lip, and across his square jaw—was clipped short and neat.

Raleigh was no stranger to half-naked men. Hell, it wasn't even the first time she'd seen August's chest since his ring gear was usually just a pair of leggings.

But the bathroom was small, he was so close, and she was slightly drunk.

And then he grinned at her, a dazzling, broad, toothy grin, and her pussy clenched.

She was in so much trouble.

Chapter Two
August

Raleigh French was in his bathroom.

THE Raleigh French. In HIS bathroom. Sure, she was *technically* here with Ben, but Ben was passed out drunk on their couch and August wasn't.

Raleigh didn't remember him, but he couldn't forget her. He'd spent four years of high school watching her. Raleigh was loud and bright and kind. She'd talk to anyone, regardless of who was in their circle of friends. She was quick-witted and smart, although August had always gotten the impression no one was supposed to know that part.

But when her boyfriend appeared, in the hallways, or the cafeteria, or the parking lot, that version of Raleigh disappeared. Snuffed out like a candle flame. Then, she was quiet. Her boyfriend wasn't very nice to her, either. He didn't like the way she kept her hair short, said her body spray smelled cheap, and her sneakers were dirty.

August had never been brave enough to say anything to her then. He was barely brave enough to say anything to her now.

But Raleigh French was practically naked on his toilet.

August's weight shifted from foot to foot and he willed his face to stay a normal shade. He was unfortunately a blusher, much to his dismay and the amusement of his peers.

He kept his gaze resolutely on her face, her slightly smudged eye liner, and stoically away from the creamy expanse of exposed thigh.

The edge of her mouth tipped up as she waited for him to do something. Or perhaps say something. Oh, yeah.

August felt the heat in his ears first as he bent to retrieve a couple clean towels and a rag from under the sink. He stacked them neatly on the edge, pushing them close to Raleigh to make sure she could reach.

"You can shower. You have to turn the knob all the way and it takes about five minutes to get hot water. Then it'll fry you up." And now he was rambling.

Raleigh glanced at the towels, still with that amused expression. "Don't suppose you have any tampons?"

"Uh, no, but I'll get some."

Her brows rose. "You'll get some?"

"Yeah."

And then he fled the bathroom, the door snicking shut in his wake. Smooth. August already had a reputation for being shy and quiet and now she was going to think he was just a regular, plain ole weirdo.

He leaned against the door and pulled his phone from the pocket of his sweats. He knew of one person who may be able to help him save the day—er, early morning.

Hey, are you up?

No

No…what?

No…I will not have sex with you

That's not, uh

Then what do you want?

Do you have any tampons?

…I knew you were a freaky little shit…

Can you bring them up?

How many you want? 5, 10, 15?

Raleigh had said it was an emergency...how many tampons constituted an emergency?

As many as you can spare

Uh, sure lol

Be right up

Thanks! You're the best!

One day I shall call in a favor, boy

August could live with that.

He suddenly found himself with sweaty palms as he waited. August glanced around the apartment, just to be sure there wasn't anything...offensive...lying about. They kept the place pretty tidy purely due to the fact that neither man had a lot of stuff and the apartment was small. Just two bedrooms and one bathroom, which Raleigh currently occupied. The massive TV was the nicest thing they owned, and weights were stacked in the dining room space in lieu of any kind of eating surface.

Ben was still passed out facedown on the couch, one of his arms dangling on the floor. August's pulse picked up as he padded to the front door, as if Ben was suddenly going to spring up and cockblock him.

Not that August knew much about cockblocking.

He didn't blame Raleigh for coming home with Ben...he doubted anyone would. He liked Ben. Ben was funny and outgoing and popular and smooth.

August wasn't even sure he could compete.

He swung the front door open on a surprised Blue, who had her fist in the air, ready to knock.

"You're quick," she said, peering around the broad expanse of his body, clearly snooping.

Blue was one of the few female wrestlers on the indie scene. He wasn't sure if Blue was her ring name or her government name; she was scrappy and tough as nails and could probably take on half the male wrestlers twice her weight in a real fight. Her hair was dyed midnight black, with bright blue streaks to match her persona.

She held up a fistful of tampons. "I only had one brand."

August felt his face heat. "I'm sure that's fine."

Her eyes flicked around his shoulders again. "You gonna tell me what's going on?"

He took the tampons. "Maybe later."

The gym was a small ecosystem...not to mention Cedar Creek the town...very little happened that wasn't widely known sooner or later anyway.

She grinned at him. "Good luck...with whatever."

"Yeah, thanks again."

She wiggled her fingers at him as he shut the door, prize secured.

The shower was still running, the bathroom door cracked as if Raleigh had opened it to let the steam out. It was just wide enough for August to snake his arm in and lay the tampons on the counter.

The shower cut off and August made a quick escape to his bedroom. There were only three doors in the tiny hallway: his room, Ben's room, and the bathroom.

He left his own door ajar, sweeping the room quickly. It was sparse, like the rest of the apartment. His bed was rumpled, but only because he had been asleep before. All his furniture matched: a dresser, one nightstand, and the bed frame. It was an outdated honey oak color that his mom had only recently found at an estate sale.

At least he had a bed frame now. Raleigh probably wouldn't have appreciated a box spring and mattress on the floor.

Not that she cared about his sleeping arrangements.

August ran a hand through his hair, ruffling the short strands. He turned towards the dresser to grab a shirt but froze.

Because Raleigh French was standing in his doorway. Her bare, red-painted toes touching his carpet.

The edges of her dark hair were wet; makeup smeared like she'd tried to wash her face but found his shower lacking. She was disheveled in a way that made his pulse race.

And she was naked.

Well, mostly naked.

She had one of August's clean, boring taupe towels wrapped around her damp, naked body. The pulse moved lower, to his dick. God, he really needed to stop thinking about her body. Stop gawking like he'd never seen a woman before in his life.

Except the towel was doing a piss-poor job at covering her thighs. It was short, and split high on her hip, like there wasn't enough fabric to go all the way around. Raleigh had a textbook pear-shaped body. Her chest was small and delicate—not that he knew what her tits looked like...it was just an assumption—while her hips and ass and thighs curved lushly together.

She had that coy smirk on her face again. It didn't seem to bother her that he was just standing there, gawking, hand outstretched towards the dresser.

"Got anything I can wear? I don't really feel like pulling that dress back on."

Chapter Three
Raleigh

August was bright pink as he stumbled towards his dresser.

"Oh, yeah, of course," he mumbled to the furniture.

He handed her a pair of black sweats and a T-shirt, his eyes landing on anything but her face. She took the clothes in one hand and adjusted her hold on the towel in the other.

August's eyes widened in panic and he quickly turned around. "Sorry." He shoved his hands into the pockets of his sweats, the movement causing the muscles of his back to ripple and contract.

His spine was a perfect chasm, bordered by lengths of lean muscle, all the way down to the perfect curve of his round ass. She had never seen a man with such a juicy ass.

It made her want to sink her teeth into it and find out what kind of sounds he would make.

He was so good and she had the strongest desire to see if he could be bad.

Grinning only to herself—because August still had his back respectfully to her—she traded the towel for his sweats and shirt. The shirt was old and frayed, *Cedar Creek High Football* emblazoned across the chest in faded white letters. It was soft as butter, in the way a well-worn shirt always was, and it smelled like him. Clean. Earthy. Thick.

She resisted bunching the fabric up and shoving it at her nose.

"Okay, I'm decent."

August's shoulders flexed, like he was releasing a relieved breath.

He turned towards her. "Here. I'll take that."

"Oh, thanks."

The used towel disappeared from her hands and August from the room, presumably to put the towel wherever it goes.

Raleigh only had a couple seconds to think of what happened next when August returned, her effects folded neatly in his hands. He set them on the top of the dresser—her thong hidden between the folds of her NYE dress and her clutch on top.

August shuffled his feet. "Do you need anything else?"

Her cramping was subsiding—the hell-hot shower helped a bit with that—but a throbbing at her temples heralded an oncoming tequila headache. How much more could she ask? She dug a toe into the carpet. "I wouldn't say no to some painkillers and some water."

His eyes lit up like there was nothing else he'd rather be doing than accommodating her.

"Yeah, yeah, obviously."

Then he was gone again, leaving her alone in his room. She heard noise from the kitchen, but he wasn't as quick this time, giving Raleigh time to observe her surroundings. They didn't tell her much about the man she saw almost every day. Except that maybe he was a minimalist.

Her inspection complete and with nothing else to do, Raleigh climbed on the bed and settled cross-legged by one of the pillows. There were only two.

August came back, ibuprofen cradled in his palm and a mug of lukewarm water. "We don't have any glasses," he said sheepishly, handing it to her.

She shrugged and threw back the pills. "Who does?" She sipped the water and then set the mug on the nightstand.

Another interaction complete. August stood with his thumbs hooked into his pockets.

She patted the bed beside her. She had no idea why she did it. Why she invited him to sit on his own damn bed with her instead of seeing if there were any rideshares in the area still running.

That was her next dilemma. She didn't drive here. They had been dropped off by a couple of guys Ben knew, one of which was still sober.

August hesitated a beat before making his decision.

He propped the other pillow against the headboard and then lay down beside her, crossing his arms and ankles. It was an exaggeratedly casual pose if she ever saw one.

She chuckled. "I won't bite." *Hard.*

A muscle feathered along his jaw. "What?"

"You don't seem very comfortable around me." Raleigh had to admit she was intrigued by that. Guys who looked like August usually had more game. That was interesting.

A red flush stole across his clavicle and one of his feet twitched. His face had almost been perpetually red since he opened the bathroom door.

She decided to change the subject. "Where were you tonight? I didn't see you at the bar."

"Oh, night off."

"And you didn't want to come out for New Year's?"

"I'm working on better sleep habits."

"Because of the special?"

He nodded, eyes finally flicking to her face and then away again just as quickly.

She plucked at the bunched fabric at her knee. "I would leave, you know, but I don't have a ride." If he didn't want her here, she wouldn't stay. That wasn't any fun.

"No!" August unfolded his body and angled his torso towards her. "I mean, no, you don't have to leave. I'm sorry I'm...weird." He had an almost panic-stricken look on his face, the short front of his hair sticking up at odd angles.

She laughed. "You're not weird." Not much. She'd met weirder, honestly.

"I'm just...nervous, I guess." He ran a hand through his hair again, the culprit, apparently, of the stuck-up strands.

"Why are you nervous? I owe you a lot right now." She held up her fingers to tick off her debts. "Hot water, your towel, tampons—I'm not even going to ask how you managed that, your clothes, ibuprofen, and water."

"I would never say you owe me anything."

She grinned. "You mean, you'd never collect on your debt?" she teased. At least, she hoped he found it teasing. She had never flirted with someone who didn't seem to be aware that they were being flirted with.

She scooted a little closer to him. Maybe she just needed to be more direct. "Wanna make out?"

Now, instead of blushing, color drained from his face. "What?" His tone was incredulous.

"I didn't get my kiss at midnight. Did you?"

She knew she was being reckless. And maybe a little bit slutty. She did come home with his roommate after all. But if August cared about that, he wasn't showing it. In fact, he was staring at her mouth, his own parted slightly. She moved again, until her knee was pressed into his thigh.

His warmth seeped through her borrowed sweats and it was so nice. She wanted to burrow into that warmth and not emerge for a very, very long time.

She leaned a little closer; August met her halfway, his eyes already closed. There was an air of genuine, sweet earnestness about him that made her feel like she could—and would—fight the world for him. To protect that sweetness, to keep him just the way he was.

She pressed her lips to his...in what was the chastest New Year's Eve kiss she'd had since she was fourteen.

August's lips were curiously closed. But then she ran the tip of her tongue along the seam, and they parted on a sigh.

Raleigh needed a better angle. She maneuvered into his lap, her knees bracketing his hips, and cupped his face.

August's eyes fluttered open, slightly dazed and still slightly panicked.

She brushed a thumb against his bottom lip. "Good?" Up so close, she noticed he had the slightest dusting of freckles across his nose and cheeks.

August nodded, his hands finally coming to brush against her hips before he tucked them between her belly and thighs.

"Kiss me again," he said.

She did, and this time August met her swipe for stroke or lick—like he'd finally given himself permission to let go.

Now it was Raleigh breathing harder, sighing into his mouth as their tongues touched. She pressed her achy breasts against his hard chest. Her nipples were hardened peaks, overly sensitive because of her period. She let her hands roam across the strong column of his throat, his collarbones, the bulging biceps she watched him hone in the gym.

August's hands stayed where he put them, but his dick was growing steadily underneath her.

Raleigh broke their kiss, and August made the cutest noise of protest. She slid further down his thighs, bracing one hand on his stone-hard pecs.

She studied the considerable bulge now tenting his sweats. Sex was off the table—she was already clean and wasn't about to make another mess, no matter how much her horny hormones protested.

She ran the tips of her fingers over his cock and August's whole body jerked.

"I'm sorry," he blurted.

His face was a flaming red that totally obscured the barely-there freckles she'd found. "For what?"

He gestured to his hard-on with his chin, like it was offending her. Nothing could be further from the truth.

Shocked, Raleigh couldn't help but laugh. Fuck, she'd protect this precious boy with her life. "You're apologizing for getting hard because I sat on your dick?" He grimaced. "Baby, I'd be offended if you didn't, honestly."

She rubbed him again, loving the way his cock jumped. He moaned, head falling back against the wall.

Raleigh pulled his sweats down just far enough to free his cock; she closed her fist around the shaft and pulled. His hips jerked and his fingers dug into the soft flesh of her upper thighs.

"Holy hell, Raleigh," he rasped.

He was almost unfairly perfect and proportionate; the perfect, silky handful. He was already leaking precum from the tip. She stroked up, running her thumb through his slit.

August's whole body shuddered, a strangled sound leaving his mouth. It was a heady feeling to watch him come apart so freely under her touch. Desire coiled in her belly, but she concentrated on the task at hand. She stroked him up and down, testing different speeds and pressures until she found one he liked, if the arch of his back was any indication.

"Raleigh, wait. Wait," he panted, closing his fist over hers.

She arched an eyebrow. "For what?"

"It's too much...I'm gonna come," he babbled adorably.

"That's the point, pretty boy." She tightened her grip, sliding her hand all the way down to the base and back up again. His own fingers tightened over hers. They stroked him together and wasn't that just hot as fuck.

August's head tilted up and his eyes were glazed and a little lost. Raleigh increased her speed. August sucked in a breath and she knew he was ready. They were both watching their hands now. He groaned as his release spurted over their fists, ropes landing on his stomach and sweatpants.

August heaved in a breath and Raleigh grinned. He let go, but she didn't, rubbing cum over the silky head of his dick until he hissed.

Then she brought two fingers to her lips, paused for half a second to enjoy the awestruck look on August's face, and then licked them clean.

Raleigh wasn't usually a swallower, mostly because men seemed to think that part of the act was owed to them and she didn't like to give them too much satisfaction. And then sometimes their cum just tasted fucking nasty and she didn't want it in her mouth any longer than necessary. But August was different. His expression was worth every swipe of her tongue, his taste just mildly salty.

With his clean hand, he grabbed her chin and crashed their mouths together again, just briefly.

"You're amazing," he said breathlessly against her lips, so softly she wasn't sure she was meant to hear it.

If he thought that was amazing, she was going to blow his mind when they fucked.

No. They were not going to fuck. She was going to have more self-control than that. This was just a New Year's Eve kiss...and a little handy. No big deal. The butterflies in her stomach were just period hormones...or possibly more cramps.

"Happy New Year," she said, hoping to break him out of the sex-drunk spell he seemed to be under.

He blinked and then smiled up at her, and it was so sweet it could break her fucking heart.

"Happy New Year."

She popped the waistband up over his softening cock. "Do you think anyone's out Ubering at this time of night?"

He huffed a laugh. "In this town? You do know you're in bumfuck, nowhere, right? It will take at least an hour to get picked up."

She sat back on his legs, ignoring the way her own body protested the lack of reciprocation. But her good sense was winning out for once.

He wiped his cum-covered hand on the sheet. "I'll drive you."

"I couldn't ask you for anything else."

"It's not a big deal. You left your car at the bar, right? Ten minutes, tops."

He was so eager to get off the bed and put a shirt and shoes on, he almost knocked her off. She laughed.

"Here you go, saving me again."

He paused in the middle of pulling on one sneaker, well-formed lips tipping down in a frown. Raleigh couldn't imagine what thoughts were causing his face to move through so many expressions at once, but it looked like he was having a lot of them.

His face settled back into something resembling neutrality and he was able to get his shoe on. What the hell was that? Surely, he didn't want her to stay? Was he having some kind of feelings about her asking to leave? Hand-jobbing and dashing? Did he think she had really traded sexual favors for a shower and some tampons?

She got off the bed and straightened her borrowed clothes. "It's cool. I'll get a ride."

"No." He caught her hand, not quite intertwining their fingers. He grinned sheepishly. "I'll just add it to your tab of favors owed."

August wasn't lying; it was only about a ten-minute drive back to the bar and it was the quietest ride of her life.

August seemed lost in his thoughts again, and Raleigh didn't feel like they had enough history to pry. They had to see each other almost every day at the gym anyway. There was no point in making the situation any more awkward than it already was.

Lights were still on in the bar and there were plenty of cars in the lot. "Party's still going, huh. Here's fine."

August stopped in front of the door and Raleigh hopped out of the truck before there could be any weird goodbyes or hemming and hawing over whether she should kiss him again. Even though she definitely wanted to.

"Raleigh."

She stopped with her hand on the door, her stuff clutched to her chest.

It was dark in the cab of the truck, the dome lights barely illuminating anything, so she couldn't see August's eyes. Just shadowy impressions of the lines of his face.

"Uh, good night," he said.

"Thanks for the lift, Callahan."

She winked at him as she shut the door and tried not to dwell too long on the odd feeling churning in her gut.

That she'd started something she couldn't finish. Or even worse—that she'd started something she wouldn't *want* to finish when the time came.

Chapter Four
August

August didn't know how he was supposed to concentrate on anything else now that he knew what Raleigh's mouth tasted like.

She stood at Teddy's elbow, looking stunning but still very professional. Her dark hair was slicked up in a neat ponytail, and her makeup was much more subdued; her thick lashes much closer to a natural length; the sweater dress covered her from neck to knee but it also hugged every sweet curve of her body.

They were in the BPC's conference room, and August had never seen so many people in the small space. There were two writers, an agent, KAIGU's talent relations manager, Teddy, Raleigh, himself, and a couple more people of whom August hadn't caught their names or roles. It was a lot.

They were finalizing his contract and storyline for the January Jam Up. Teddy wasn't his agent or manager, in the traditional sense, but he had been in the business forever and could ferret out bad contracts.

August's contract was in front of him. The talent manager had briefed them on the legalities included, but Teddy still insisted on reading every word.

August was thankful. Since he couldn't currently think straight, he'd missed half of what the manager had said already.

Teddy tapped a pen against his chin and slid the stack of papers over to August. "It's a good contact. A four-match storyline." One of Teddy's thick fingers tapped a figure. August's salary.

He inhaled and wiped sweaty palms against his thighs. It was more money than August's bank account had ever seen before. He'd get paid in four installments, one after each match.

It wasn't professional money, but it was *good* money for him, a virtual nobody from the indie circuit.

KAIGU was the biggest promotion in their region. If he could make a name for himself there, there was a good chance of being scouted for the bigger promotions.

One of the writers was speaking, a slight man that August vaguely recognized. He was probably a retired performer. "It's a tag team match with one of our veterans. You'll get your ass kicked for most of the match and then save the day. And then you'll do three more tag team matches. If the audience likes you, we can extend your contact and storyline."

August glanced at Teddy, who nodded.

"Yeah, that sounds great. Who's my partner?"

"Joel Nelson. He's one of our favorite babyfaces. Very wholesome, clean cut. Good guy. You'll fit right in."

The talent manager laughed. "Don't change anything between now and taping, right?"

"Oh, of course not," August said.

"Your ring name is just August?" A writer again.

August nodded. The two writers glanced at each other, and one began scribbling in the notebook in front of him.

"We'll brainstorm that, yeah?"

"Uh, okay." August had been brainstorming his ring name since he was seven years old. He hadn't really been able to come up with something else. He was always just himself and didn't know if he wanted to be anyone else.

"And you're single, right?" The talent manager again.

August could feel his face go bright red. Great. "I'm not sure why that's relevant." God, was it in his contract?

"Better for potential storylines," a writer said.

"Single, good-looking new talent performs better with our female audience, we've found," said the talent manager with a wink.

August felt his pulse in his ears. "Yeah, I'm single."

Another note, another wink, some jokes and laughs. It was too much. The room was too small, stifling. August's throat suddenly felt dry. Was he having some kind of anxiety attack? It had been years since he'd felt such a suffocating pressure in his gut.

A water bottle was placed on the table in front of him, and slender but firm fingers squeezed the back of his neck. Raleigh's chest brushed against his shoulder as she moved on to hand out the next bottle of water.

Was it so obvious he was losing his shit? Out of his depth?

"I don't think changing his ring name is the best move," she said casually on her route around the room. "Almost half a million followers know him as just August."

That was true. And it wasn't because of him. His attempts at social media were half-assed, at best. Harper Myles made that happen. She knew what the people wanted. Which apparently was gym workouts and thirst traps of him sweaty and slicked up in just his gear.

There were more thoughtful looks and some pen scratching.

Teddy nodded. "She's right. You wanted him as-is, with the audience he already has. Why change something that's working?"

August felt relief wash over him and the muscles in his neck loosened.

The KAIGU producer nodded. "True enough. You were always the savviest in the business, Teddy." They guffawed and Raleigh—who was standing behind the producer—rolled her eyes. It wasn't super obvious—she was too professional for that—and August doubted anyone else would have noticed unless they were also watching her as intently as he was. And then she grinned, and the smile was just for him. Like it was their secret.

Their official business concluded, the conversations devolved into industry news and gossip. August felt like it was a good time to excuse himself from the room. He was already late for the day's workout, and he was on at the bar tonight.

He had almost made it to the locker room before he heard the click of heels on the floor behind him.

Raleigh was there, clipboard in hand. "You forgot to sign your contract."

What an idiot move, you dumbass.

"Oh, yeah, thanks," he said, because he couldn't think of anything smoother to say.

She handed him a pen and pointed to the correct spots with one of her long, glittery nails that were shaped like tiny coffins. He remembered how those nails felt scraping against his skin and shivered and hoped she didn't notice. It had only been a few days since New Year's Eve and he hadn't really talked to her since, even though it felt like he was slowly dying. He didn't know what to say. He didn't know how to act.

So, it was just back to his default. Quiet weirdo.

He signed, and Raleigh took the pen back, the pads of her fingers brushing his.

"Hey." She grasped his chin—because he had averted his eyes, *again*. She was shorter than him normally, but in her boots they were almost eye to eye. Her hand slid up, so his chin was resting perfectly in the curve between her thumb and forefinger. It felt like it belonged there. "Don't let some tight-butthole pencil-pushers change you if you don't want to be changed. You're the star, remember?"

Making it big, being called up into the big leagues, being able to wrestle professionally, was August's dream. It was what he worked for. But it still felt so far away. He didn't feel like a star. Except, when Raleigh said it, when she looked at him like that, he could actually believe it.

"You work tonight?" She released his chin, all business again.

He nodded, throat tight. He couldn't handle her being so close. He could feel the heat radiating from her body...or maybe that was just his own anxiety.

Her soft gray eyes sparkled, crinkling at the corners as she smiled. "See ya later, maybe."

She sauntered away, back towards the front office and the conference room, and August continued down the hallway to the lockers. Most of the lockers were first come first serve for the gym-goers, but there was a small, reserved section for the regular guys.

August beelined for his locker, already pulling his shirt over his head.

"Goose," a loud voice boomed from the showers.

Ben came around the corner, a towel slung low on his hips, his curly hair damp and sticking to his shoulders.

Ben was the only person who called August "Goose" because he liked to pronounce his name as *Augoost*, with a long O, when they were dicking around.

"You're late," he said, banging open his own locker, which was right next to August's.

"Meeting with KAIGU."

Ben sucked air in through his teeth. "Nice. They gonna pay a pretty penny?"

August flushed. "Yeah, man."

Ben socked him on the shoulder. "We're all rooting for you, man. Livin' the dream." Ben flashed his signature dazzling smile.

They hadn't really spoken much since New Year's. Did Ben know he and Raleigh had...hung out? Was that breaking some kind of bro code? August had never done really well deciphering bro code.

If Ben was upset, he wasn't letting on, but August still felt odd. Like he was keeping some kind of big secret from one of his closest friends.

August pulled a pair of shorts from his locker. Ben was putting on fresh deodorant and gel in his hair.

"Hey," August started, "are you okay with Raleigh?"

Ben snorted. "I think I need more words than that, man."

Right. That question was about as clear as mud. What should he tell him? August could feel his face heating again. He didn't want to tell Ben about everything that transpired in his room. It was a moment shared between him and Raleigh.

"Uh, well, we talked, after you passed out, on New Year's."

Ben waggled his eyebrows. "Talked, huh? Is that what the kids are calling it these days?"

"No, we didn't—"

Ben smacked him on the shoulder again before grabbing his own clean clothes. "It's cool, bro. Happy for you. She's great. Hot." Then he was ditching his towel in the hamper and pulling on his shorts. "I might bump you harder out there, though, just for the cockblock."

"You were out cold," August protested.

Ben laughed as he sauntered out of the locker room. "Doesn't matter!" he threw back over his shoulder.

August shook his head. He could handle a few friendly, retaliatory bumps in the ring.

He and Ben were good, and he might get to see Raleigh again at the bar tonight. Would she show? Or was she just being nice to him? Did she feel sorry for him because he'd been alone on New Year's Eve? Was he her second choice, a consolation prize since Ben was unavailable?

Raleigh didn't strike him as the kind of person who was intentionally cruel. And she defended him in the conference room earlier.

She didn't have to speak up for him like that. That had to mean something.

August changed quickly. He needed to get into the ring, or get under a weight rack, and quiet the misgivings running through his head.

She'd show tonight or she wouldn't.

Chapter Five
Raleigh

Raleigh was no stranger to the bar. There wasn't anywhere else to go, and she wasn't driving thirty or forty minutes for a drink on a weeknight.

So, why did she feel nervous tonight?

She didn't have to go. She could just go home, put her pajamas on, and watch some juicy reality TV while eating chocolate drizzled popcorn.

August was working.

It wasn't like this was a date. Because she didn't date people she worked with.

She didn't owe him anything. She hadn't promised him anything.

And yet.

And yet she'd touched up her makeup and swapped her sweater dress for a patent leather mini skirt and a cropped sweater that still worked with her tights and boots.

Harper was busy, but Raleigh showed up anyway. Odds were there would be someone there she could talk to for a couple hours while she nursed her drink.

Noise bubbled around her as the door swung shut. Whoever had control of the music was currently playing some kind of boppy number that was really out of sync with the whole vibe of the place.

She didn't see August at first when she approached the bar. It was manned by one of the other, full-time bartenders, an older guy named Leon who may have lived in Cedar Creek since its founding. He was an institution. She couldn't remember a time when she didn't see Leon at the grocery store or at church, when that was something her mother could still make her do.

"Leon," she greeted, sliding up onto a stool and crossing her legs, so she would appear exceedingly casual.

"Miss Raleigh," he returned, like he'd been greeting her for at least twenty years. "Out hunting tonight?" He grinned at her, showing at least three gold teeth.

Raleigh flipped her hair. "I don't have to hunt, Leon. They come to me, remember?"

He snorted. "So, can I get you a drink, or are we waiting for prey?" The thought of tequila kind of made her stomach turn, but she was too slow. "And none of that fancy shit."

"Fineeeeee. Angry Orchard, please."

"I said nothin' fancy," he complained, but walked away to get her a bottle anyway.

Raleigh scanned the room quickly; there was a rowdy group by the pool tables but no August had materialized yet. He had said he was working tonight, right? She hadn't made that up?

Leon came back with an Angry Orchard and slid it across the bar to her with a grumble.

"You by yourself tonight?" She tipped the bottle to her lips. She was casual. So casual.

Leon speared her with a beady-eyed glare, all the deep lines on his weathered face deepening. She wanted to clutch her pearls; she had never seen such a look. Well, had never seen such a look directed at her.

"Y'all need to leave that boy alone."

"Y'all?" Raleigh glanced around; she was currently the only patron seated at the bar. "Who's y'all?"

He jabbed a gnarled finger at her. "You girls. Hangin' around here like vultures. I'm gonna start chargin' y'all a fee for lookin'. That boy is goin' places." His finger swerved to point at a calendar on the back wall, where August's TV debut was circled. "He don't need no distractions or fuckin' kids."

Raleigh choked on her cider. "Jesus, Leon."

"I know the type."

"Not me."

"Your momma was."

It wasn't said with much vitriol, but Raleigh felt the sting of Leon's words anyway. It was a poorly kept secret that her mom had gotten pregnant so that her dad would have to leave his wife—a dewy-eyed prom queen and state pageant winner. The whole debacle had been *dramatic*, and Raleigh still felt the repercussions even now. Her mom was a fucking meteor, destroying lives and leaving wide swathes of damage in her wake.

It had worked for a couple years, though. Her dad had in fact left his first wife, married Raleigh's mom, and they had a few miserable years together before he left town forever.

Raleigh tipped her bottle. "Touché."

She would never admit the accusation stung, even though she had no desire to have kids, like, ever. She was pretty sure her uterus was busted anyway.

She had no plans to baby-trap poor August, but she felt an uncomfortable surge of guilt that had her leaving her place at the bar. She didn't want a relationship, so what the fuck was she doing here waiting on him?

Yes, he was a fucking fantastic kisser. And yes, okay, she could definitely get used to the way he looked at her. Like she was the only girl in the entire world. Like she was worth something. Like she meant something. Like she might mean something to him.

It was a heady combo. A stupid combo.

"Well, look who the cat dragged in."

She had wandered closer to the pool tables and drawn the attention of one of the guys. She hadn't realized he was there, and his exaggerated hick drawl sent unpleasant goose bumps up her arms.

She didn't bother to contain her eye roll. "Cameron."

They had gone out a few times, hooked up a few times, but it didn't take long for Cameron's true colors to come shining through.

He swaggered closer, leaning against his pool stick like that made him look cool. He wore designer ripped jeans and a T-shirt that was too tight; his backwards ball cap topped light blond curls that were way too nice for such an asshole. He didn't deserve nice hair.

His eyes raked over her from head to toe, and the look made her skin crawl.

"I've been looking for you."

She sipped her cider. "Have you?"

"I didn't think we were finished yet."

"You finished. I never did."

The other men around them—his buddies, she presumed, though she didn't know most of their names—guffawed.

Cameron didn't like that. His mouth thinned, hand flexing on the pool stick. "I didn't hear you complaining."

"We all make mistakes sometimes, Cameron." She saluted him with her bottle, set it on the edge of the pool table, and turned on her heel. It was time to go home. She wasn't drunk enough to deal with his bullshit.

She almost made it to the door.

Two arms wrapped around her middle and swung her body around, so she faced the men at the pool tables again. Cameron laughed the entire time, like they were both in on the joke.

"A girl as pretty as you shouldn't leave so early, yeah?" His hot breath wafted over her face, and she could smell the cheap beer. Raleigh's stomach swooped.

She tried to push him off her, but Cameron just tightened his arms, one of his hands creeping under her sweater.

"Let me go."

Most of the bystanders were still laughing, or turning to resume their game, unconcerned with whatever Cameron had in mind. To his credit, one guy did look mildly concerned.

"Hey, man," he started, but Cameron just laughed louder, swaying against her back like they were going to dance.

"She's fine. Aren't you, baby?"

"No," she said, and was ignored again in favor of more groping.

Raleigh started a countdown in her head. She'd give him three seconds before causing a scene.

One.

Two.

Three.

"Did you not fucking hear her?"

The music had cut out so the whole bar heard August Callahan say "fucking" and Raleigh wasn't sure what was more shocking: the profanity, or the fact that he was rounding the bar and headed straight for them.

Cameron didn't let her go; his fingers brushed the skin of her abdomen, and she stomped on his foot. He cursed and finally released her. "Jesus, fuck, fine."

August was still approaching, two dark spots of color high on his cheeks. He must have been in the kitchen; he had a black apron slung low on his waist and his T-shirt was damp and sticking to his abs.

"You need to leave, dude."

Cameron rolled his eyes and adjusted his ball cap. "Are you gonna make me?" He was still grinning, but none of his boys were joining in this time. The joke wasn't so funny anymore.

August planted his feet and squared his shoulders. "If I need to."

Cameron laughed. "Yeah fucking right. You couldn't take a real punch, you fucking pussy."

Both men were almost touching chests now, Cameron not stepping back even though August had him by a couple inches and probably thirty pounds. The confidence of drunk white men.

August seemed disturbingly calm in comparison to Cameron's flared nostrils and heaving breaths. Was he going to just stand there and let him hit him? August's calmness appeared to infuriate Cameron.

"That's what I thought, fucking pussy." Then he shoved August in the chest, hard.

August stepped back with one foot to keep his balance, absorbing the movement like it was nothing. His fists clenched and a muscle feathered in his jaw.

This was getting ridiculous. And she was about to do something stupid.

"Okay, that's enough." Raleigh pushed herself between the two men, hands held up like a fucking referee. She caught August's gaze and an unwanted, fuzzy feeling filled her gut at how pissed off he looked. She grinned at him. "You're the star, remember? Gotta protect that pretty face."

Then she turned to Cameron. And punched him in the face.

It hurt.

"Oh, fuck."

"You fucking bitch."

"You lot better get the fuck out of my bar before I beat the shit outta ya. And it'll hurt a lot worse than some sucker punch from a girl. No, not you, you get back in the kitchen and get the girl some ice."

Cameron and his boys scattered as Leon came around the bar with a baseball bat that looked like it had definitely been used before.

Raleigh was holding her wrist and breathing through her nose. She felt...energized. Like she could run a marathon or punch more boys despite the current throbbing of her hand.

Leon pointed his bat at her. "You, sit down."

She practically skipped to the bar; her cheeks hurt from grinning.

"Don't look so happy about it," Leon grumbled.

"I've been *dying* to fight a man."

Leon snorted. "That one was barely a man."

He brought her another Angry Orchard just as August reappeared with a plastic baggie of ice and a dish rag.

The blush on his face had spread across his cheekbones. It was adorable. "It's clean."

He held out his hand, palm up. Raleigh grabbed her new cider and slid her sore hand into August's. His thumb gently ran across her red knuckles; she wanted to shiver from the pleasure of it, the warmth.

August covered the back of her hand with the rag and then placed the ice. He didn't let go of her hand. His mouth quirked. "Your form needs some work."

"I know, right? He didn't even bleed." Which was probably a good thing, in hindsight, but boy would it have been satisfying to see Cameron with a bloody nose.

Now, August frowned, like he was disappointed with her. A cute little furrow appeared between his brows.

"You shouldn't have put yourself between us."

"Why not?"

"You could have gotten hurt."

She grinned and tipped her chin towards her sore hand he was cradling. "Well, kinda did that anyway, huh."

"It could've been worse."

"I couldn't let you get a busted lip. KAIGU wouldn't be happy."

There was hollering from the kitchen and August glanced over his shoulder. "Will you, uh, can you wait for me to get off?"

She should tell him no. Let him down easy while she still could. It was the perfect excuse. It probably wouldn't even feel like a rejection at this point; it was only natural for her to go home. But his big fingers were still curled around her hand.

"What time?"

"Eleven."

"Yeah, okay."

Chapter Six
August

He half-suspected Raleigh just said yes to waiting on him to be nice, but she actually waited for him to get off work.

It was a weeknight, which meant the bar was relatively slow and closed several hours earlier than the weekend shifts.

Raleigh didn't just wait at the bar, though. She iced her hand, as instructed, for only ten minutes and then abandoned her post to go play pool. Then, an older couple came in that she must've known and she went and sat with them, shooting the shit until closing time.

She was fascinating to watch and August found his eyes drawn to her whenever he left the kitchen. She was so vibrant, so assured, so confident. What must it feel like, to command a room so effortlessly? August still felt like a gangly, unwieldy teenager, even though it had been years since those days and his body was very different now. Built and carefully sculpted.

Her dark ponytail swung animatedly as she laughed; it rocked with the rhythm of her hips as she strutted around the bar like she owned it. She was covered from head to toe except for the tiny sliver of stomach he glimpsed every once in a while.

That only served to remind him of Cameron's hand up her sweater earlier. August had never felt the urge to *actually* hit someone until that moment. If Raleigh hadn't done it, he would have instead, the KAIGU contract be damned.

Leon swatted him on the back of the head with a towel. "You'd get done faster if you'd stop rubbernecking."

August's face flamed and he bent down to focus on his tasks: cleaning the grill and fryers.

When he was done, he was sweaty and smelled quite strongly of fried chicken. He said good night to Leon and the other staff, pulled his hoodie over his damp and dirty shirt, and found Raleigh waiting for him in the empty front room. She was leaning against the frame of the front door, back arched in a way that looked simultaneously too casual and too fucking tempting.

She brightened when she saw him, pushing off the frame. "All done?"

"Yeah." His pulse was racing. Why had he asked her to wait, again? Oh, yeah, cause he was an infatuated dumb-ass.

She fell into step beside him, her shoulder brushing his arm (was that on purpose?) as they walked to the parking lot.

"I'm over here." She gestured towards a small compact.

"Is your hand okay?"

She held it up for his inspection, flexing her fingers. The skin was a little red across her knuckles, but that was the worst of it.

"I'll probably be ready for more punching in a day or two."

He huffed. "You probably shouldn't." He stuffed his hands in his pockets and tried not to shuffle his feet. What now? *What is the plan, August?*

Raleigh was watching him, her way-too-perceptive gaze raking over him, noting his shuffling and his blush. God, he wished he were someone different in this moment. Someone who knew what the fuck to do.

She gave him a small smile, just a slight lift of her mouth that caused a dimple to pop in her cheek. Shit, she was beautiful.

"Was there something else, August?" She had lowered her voice into something dark and sultry, lashes fluttering as her gaze dropped to his mouth.

His chest constricted. He cleared his suddenly dry throat. He could do this. "I, uh, I wanted to kiss you. Again." That didn't even touch the depth of his *want* but it would be enough for now.

Another small smile, a step towards him. She was close enough to touch.

"Then kiss me," she said.

August's breath shuddered out. Raleigh waited. He remembered earlier that day, when she'd gripped his chin, the way that touch had made him feel. Would she like that?

He squeezed his fists so tight he could feel his nails pressing into his palms. But then he took his hands out of his pockets. Flexed his fingers.

Brought one hand up and cupped her jaw. She had a nice, defined jawline, strong. He tightened his grip infinitesimally and her lips parted.

Her breath was warm on his face as he tipped her head up. He took one more inhale before crashing their mouths together. It was almost as if touching her skin, seeing her reaction, broke something timid inside him.

Raleigh moaned softly and sagged against him, her hands clutching at his hoodie. He held her chin firmly, supporting her body with his other hand on her hip.

He kissed her the only way he knew how: like he needed her to breathe. She was warm and pliant under him, her mouth opening without hesitation.

His hand moved from her hip to the small of her back and down, until it rested on the swell of her ass.

"Go home, kids." Leon's raspy bellow echoed across the mostly empty lot.

Raleigh laughed, breaking their contact, but only barely. Her lips still brushed his. And she had a tight hold on his hoodie.

"Do you want to come home with me?"

He had never wanted anything more in his entire life. Not even wrestling. Not even the temporary contract with KAIGU. August's heart hammered against his ribs like a rabbit's, the beat frantic. He should tell her, right? Now would be the moment, right?

Raleigh waited patiently, her storm-cloud gray eyes almost black in the dark parking lot.

He rubbed a circle in the small of her back. "Yes."

She smiled and pecked him on the lips. "Follow me, then."

Raleigh lived in a complex of condominiums, some owned and some rented, off Hickory Hollow Road.

There was a patio entrance and what looked like a front entrance through a mailroom. She led him across the grass to the patio, which was empty except for a few potted plants that looked like they'd seen better days.

August tried not to follow too closely, just in case she changed her mind and told him to go home.

She didn't.

She let him in her house.

She toed off her boots on the small rug and spread her arms wide. "Ta da."

It…wasn't exactly what he was expecting. He pulled off his own shoes. "Where's your furniture?"

The condo space was open concept like most things were these days. He could see in the small kitchen. There was no furniture in the space he could see. No chairs, no couches, no TV, no dining room table.

"I'm still working on that." She winked at him over her shoulder. "Do you want something to drink? Beer? Hard liquor?"

The surprise of Raleigh's empty condo had chased the nerves away. He was still looking at the empty walls. "I don't drink."

She peeked around the small wall that led to the kitchen. "You work in a bar and don't drink?"

"Alcohol is not part of the diet I'm on."

"Oh." He heard some clinking as Raleigh presumably rummaged around the fridge. "I guess that makes sense. KAIGU wants to get what they paid for."

She came back in view and slid two Cokes over the bar.

"Was that meeting...normal?" Their meeting with the promotion had been bothering him all day.

She popped her tab. "What about it?"

He took the other can, rubbing his thumb over the lip. "You know, the stipulation that I have to be single."

She shrugged. "It's not the weirdest thing I've heard about, honestly. They're not exactly wrong about it. It's easier to create storylines around you if you're not already spoken for. So much opportunity for drama." She sipped and he watched the slide of her throat.

The nerves came flooding back with a new vengeance. His hand was almost shaking as he set his unopened Coke back down on the counter.

"Wanna see the bedroom?"

If Raleigh noticed anything amiss, she wasn't showing it. She flipped her ponytail over her shoulder and walked down a barely-there hallway.

August's nerves fired like he'd just chugged a pot of coffee, but he didn't drink caffeine anymore because it wasn't on his diet. The jittery rumble under his skin was just because he was in Raleigh's bedroom.

Her bedroom was a marked difference from the rest of the condo, but all he got was a brief impression of *more stuff* because Raleigh sat on the edge of her bed and crossed her legs. She leaned back on her hands. The position splayed her thighs and exposed a small roll of her belly.

He wanted to bite that bit of ivory skin. In fact, he wanted to taste all of her, lick all of her.

He approached the bed.

Raleigh uncrossed her legs and he stepped between her spread thighs, the motion pushing her short skirt up even higher. There was a tiny flush across her cheeks. She leaned up, her hands immediately going to his ass; she squeezed proprietarily, and he could almost feel her nails through his jeans.

August ran a hand through her silky hair as she pressed her nose to his abdomen.

He huffed a laugh. "I probably smell like fried chicken."

Her hands slid under his shirt and hoodie, pushing them both up. "I like fried chicken."

Then her hot tongue was on his stomach. August couldn't hold in his gasp. His dick strained against his zipper so hard it hurt. It had to be painfully noticeable to Raleigh. It was probably sticking her in the throat.

She licked her way over every ridge of his abs, across and down, until she hit the waistband of his jeans.

He groaned, leaning into the touch; he felt her hands fumbling with the button of his jeans. August struggled to control his breathing, but it felt impossible, like the last rep of a deadlift set. Last time she had only used her hands, but she had his pants open and her hot mouth was kissing over his briefs.

His balls drew up painfully. Shit, he was gonna come in his underwear and she hadn't even taken them off yet.

"Uh, wait." The words left his mouth in a breathy whisper.

But Raleigh heard them and tipped her head back, keeping her grip on his hips. Her lips were damp and pleasantly swollen.

His throat was dry. He could do this. "I want to...taste you." His eyes flicked down her still clothed body, hoping she got his meaning. He should have been more direct and not used the stupid euphemism.

Raleigh grinned. "Well, why didn't you say so sooner?"

She stripped with an enthusiasm August felt he didn't deserve since he had never done this. She was down to her underwear—a mismatched bra and panties. Her underwear was a pretty floral pattern with a tiny bow right under her belly button while the bra was black lace. The cups were cut low, showcasing the small swells of her tits.

She crawled back on the bed and cocked one knee up, laying herself out for his purview like a meal.

Ignoring his painful bulge, August shucked his jeans so he'd be more comfortable. He pressed one knee into the bed, between Raleigh's long, slender feet.

Her eyes glittered in the low light as she let both thighs fall apart. She tucked her hands behind her head, waiting.

Blood thundered through August's body, loud in his ears and pulsing in his temples. He stroked her thick, soft thighs, and felt the muscles twitch under his palms.

He hooked his fingers in the waistband of her panties, and she lifted her hips so he could pull them down; he helped her guide one leg free.

And then she was exposed beneath him.

She was gorgeous and perfect, the dark hair on her mound springy and spry, the skin of her lips just slightly darker than everywhere else; she was wet there, already.

Raleigh released a breathless laugh. "You're looking at me like you've never seen pussy before."

Now. He needed to tell her now. And if it got him kicked out, so be it. "I've never...done...this before."

Raleigh frowned, her dark brows almost touching in the middle. She pushed up on her elbows. "Done what? Eaten a girl out?"

He swallowed. His hands were still on her knees, and he never wanted to let go. He squeezed her gently. "Any of it."

"It? Any of what?"

"Sex. I've never had sex." There. That wasn't so hard.

Raleigh's face went slack. "You're a virgin?" Her expression quickly morphed into horror. "New Year's...when we...was that...that wasn't? The first time..." She trailed off, like she couldn't quite articulate her horror and concern.

"I've jacked off, Raleigh. I've fooled around before, just never gone all the way."

It didn't feel like that big of a deal to August anymore, but it always was to other people, to the point where he just stopped talking about it. His guy friends always assumed he got laid thoroughly because of the way girls tended to fawn and flirt with him, even though he seemed mostly incapable of flirting back. If he was being honest with himself, he'd never really had a strong urge to have sex with anyone. But that was probably weird.

He'd never had an official girlfriend before either, so there had been no one before Raleigh to tell.

Not that she was his girlfriend or anything like that. He knew better. *Just wishful thinking.*

Raleigh tried to wiggle her hips away from him, but that wasn't what he wanted at all. He firmed up his grip. "No."

"August, I haven't...I don't think this is a good idea." She bit her lip.

Was she insane? This was the best idea August had ever had. Raleigh's sudden hesitation made him feel bolder, gave him a little more balls. She wanted him to prove to her that he wanted her more than anything? He would prove that to her.

"Teach me," he said. "Teach me how to make you come. God, I wanna watch you come."

Her lips parted, a subtle flush creeping down her neck. She nodded.

"Can I take off your bra?"

She nodded again, leaning towards him so the back clasps were within reach. He snapped them open with one hand and that made her laugh.

"Done that before, have you?"

He smiled, feeling some of the earlier tension bleed out from between them. "Didn't say I was some kind of pristine altar boy."

The bra straps fell down her shoulders and she shrugged it off, tossing it to the floor.

Finally.

August hadn't just been imagining that she had perfect tits. She actually did. They were small but perky, the nipples rosy points that made his mouth water. He may have actually started drooling. He wanted to taste all of her, run his tongue over every inch of flesh. Worship her body with his mouth and hands until she was delirious.

She laid back down.

"Take your hair tie out," he said.

Her lips twitched. "I thought I was teaching?"

He flushed, but Raleigh had already pulled the tie out of her glossy hair, and it spilled across the pillows like dark water.

She settled into the bed, hands up by her face, eyes slightly hooded. August loomed over her, his knee dangerously close to the hottest part of her body.

He leaned down, his breath ghosting over the line of her jaw. "Can I kiss you?"

"That's a good start," she sighed.

He started with a soft spot right under her chin, kissing his way to the hollow of her throat. Her skin was impossibly soft and tasted like vanilla.

Vanilla. It was the same scent that wafted off her when they were teenagers.

He liked the way her breathing quickened with every touch of his lips or flick of his tongue.

He trailed a path down her sternum, sucking on the side of one of her breasts. When his mouth closed over her nipple, she arched into his mouth with a soft moan that made his dick twitch. He wasn't sure how much pressure to use; he didn't want to mark her skin. But the harder he sucked, the more Raleigh whimpered and writhed under him.

"Oh, fuck," she gasped as he licked her nipple. He felt her hand on the back of his neck, urging him farther down. "Down, down, go down," she panted.

August couldn't help but grin against her stomach as he followed her directions. He slid off the edge of the bed, hooking his hands into the crevices at her hips and dragging her body down the bed with him. She yelped at the sudden movement but then laughed in a breathy way that he liked. She was usually so cool, so controlled, so measured and composed, and her laugh felt like something free.

He was eye level with her pussy, and he felt like maybe he shouldn't feel intimidated, but he did. He'd been in locker rooms all his life and heard all sorts of things men said about how hard it was to please a woman. How difficult they were. How most of them just faked it anyway.

The last thing he wanted to do was disappoint her, or to make her feel like she had to fake it for his benefit. His ego wasn't that fragile.

His cheek brushed along the inside of her thigh. He wanted to stroke her so that's what he did. With two fingers, he spread her open, exposing her swollen clit. That's where he put his mouth and sucked.

Raleigh's hips bucked and she made a choked sound. "Slow down, pretty boy."

"Okay. I can do that."

Raleigh chuckled, her thighs gently shivering around his ears.

With his thumb, August stroked her slowly, up and down, circling her clit, keeping the pressure light until she was squirming.

"Harder, now, now."

August rubbed her clit directly now, harder and faster, listening to the cadence of her moans, the hitch of her breathing.

"Yes, fuck, yes. Mouth, mouth, mouth," she chanted.

August replaced his fingers with his mouth, his tongue following the path his thumb had just taken. Her thighs locked around his head and he took that as a good sign.

"Fuck me with your fingers."

His middle finger slid inside her hot channel with ease. She was so wet.

He felt her walls flutter while her hips bore down on his face and finger.

She whined. "Another, fuck."

He inserted another and felt her clamp around him. Her thighs were quaking and he couldn't describe the sounds coming out of her mouth, but they made his dick throb where it was pressed against the mattress.

He worked his fingers in and out of her dripping pussy, trying to keep up the same pace with his tongue on her pulsing clit.

She gripped the back of his head with surprising force, shoving his face deeper into her sweet heat.

He felt gluttonous, his wants and desires like a hole in his chest that would never be filled. Not until he had Raleigh, had all parts of her, over and over and over again.

She came on a strangled scream, her whole body seizing and quivering, her juices practically dripping off his chin.

He kissed her clit, her mound, the inside of her smooth thigh before joining her on the bed. Her chest was heaving, eyes closed, a sheen of sweat on her forehead.

"That was your first time doing that?"

August touched his wet lips. "Yeah."

Raleigh's mouth moved, but she didn't make any sound. It kind of looked like she'd mouthed "wow," but that could also just be his ego making things up.

She rolled towards him suddenly, grabbing his mouth in a hungry kiss. She'd be able to taste herself. His erection was a painful ache as it pressed against her thigh. He knew he was spreading precum over her flushed skin. He couldn't help it. And he couldn't find it in himself to regret it. He wanted her covered with him.

His hips twitched of their own accord. He felt her smile against his lips and then her slender fingers wrapped around his hot shaft.

It was embarrassing, how close to the edge he was already. It only took a couple firm strokes, her tongue in his mouth, her teeth nipping his bottom lip, and then he was spilling over both their abdomens.

They were both breathing hard in the silent bedroom. Raleigh rolled onto her back again.

"Now, we talk," she said, her tone leaving no room for argument.

August groaned.

He didn't want to talk.

He'd gotten a taste of her and now he wanted it all.

Chapter Seven
Raleigh

August Callahan ate pussy like a man starving.

It was quite possibly the best orgasm of her life; she'd seen stars.

It was almost good enough for Raleigh to forget what he'd confessed before he went down on her.

August Callahan was a virgin.

Sweet, earnest, wide-eyed wrestling prodigy August was a true-blue virgin. In hindsight, it explained a lot of his awkwardness around her. Would he stop blushing every time he saw a wrist now that he'd had his tongue in her cunt? She kind of hoped not. She liked that about him. She didn't want him to change.

Did men think about virginity the same way a lot of her friends did? Raleigh'd gotten rid of hers at the earliest opportunity. It made women stupid. Clouded their judgement. Got them stuck in situations they couldn't escape.

But she was still stuck in the same small town she'd grown up in so maybe she was just as stupid as everyone else too.

August shifted on the bed, bringing her back to their current predicament.

His cum was drying tacky on her stomach. "Be right back. And then we'll talk."

It was a huge test of her willpower to leave a very naked, flushed, semi-hard August on her bed and go get a couple of warm rags. She cleaned her stomach off in the bathroom and brought the other back to August.

His dark, hooded eyes tracked her around the bed. She tossed the rag and it thwacked him in the chest.

She grabbed a moderately clean oversized T-shirt from the pile in the laundry chair and tugged it on before joining him on the bed again, pulling the shirt over her knees.

August frowned as he absently wiped the rag half-heartedly across his abs. "You put your clothes back on." His tone bordered on petulant and Raleigh wanted to smile. But this was serious.

Where to start?

"Okay, so why are you still a virgin?"

Excellent.

August opened his mouth, closed it, tipped his head. Turned his body towards her, propped his head on his palm. Which did absolutely nothing to keep Raleigh on task.

"It just...never happened, I guess?"

"Is that a question?"

He smiled, and color slashed on his cheekbones. "I was a weird kid, a bit of a loner. My family didn't have a lot growing up. My mom worked a lot. I watched a lot of wrestling on TV by myself. Once I discovered weightlifting, I spent a lot of time in the gym." He cocked his head, as if gathering his thoughts. "I just went so long, and it never felt important, really. Not as important as trying to make something of myself, to work, to help my mom."

"You never had any interest in anyone? Girls? Or boys?"

"In case you haven't noticed...I'm horrible with girls."

"But, you're, like, really attractive. You wouldn't even need to talk that much, honestly."

He sighed and fell back on the bed, putting one big hand on his rigid abdomen and one behind his head. "I haven't always looked this way, you know."

"You went to Cedar Creek High, didn't you? What year? I don't remember you."

One of his brows arched. "You wouldn't, would you? I was a skinny nobody. I didn't have any friends. We didn't have any money for extracurriculars. Poor white trash."

That, Raleigh could relate to. "White trash tends to stick together."

"Not when they're pretty."

"You remember me?"

"Sure." He smiled at the ceiling as if recalling a fond memory. "You wore stripper heels to graduation."

Raleigh let out a peal of delighted laughter. "Oh my God. I did, didn't I? My mom thought they were nice."

Raleigh remembered almost tripping down the stairs as she left the stage because she'd insisted on the seven-inch heels with rhinestone bottoms. Would have served her right to bust her ass. She'd held on to those shoes for so long even though she'd never worn them again, just because they cost almost a hundred dollars. And she couldn't just throw that kind of money away.

They were totally frivolous, but her mom had been feeling generous, and maybe a little proud she'd actually made it to graduation.

"You should have seen my dress."

August grinned at her. "Did it match the shoes?"

"Pretty close." She leaned down to grab the chunky throw blanket that they'd dislodged from the foot of her bed, dragging it over both their legs.

August's brow furrowed, but he didn't protest. She noticed dark circles getting more pronounced under his eyes. Their seven a.m. meeting with KAIGU felt like a lifetime ago.

She snuggled a little closer to get more blanket and he adjusted his body so she could fit right under his arm, like it was the most natural thing in the world. Like she belonged there. She adjusted her hair so it wasn't in her face and pressed her cheek to his chest.

"Where'd you go? After graduation?"

Raleigh had gone nowhere. She worked odd job after odd job until she landed with Teddy. She couldn't remember seeing August around town before he started showing up at the gym.

"Tennessee, mostly. To X-Treme Impact."

Raleigh knew about X-Treme Impact Tennessee. She knew most of the small, independent promotions in the region. They were like the BPC: finding and developing talent, running their own shows, hoping to have guys called up into the professional promotions.

"You got out and came back?"

His chest vibrated with laughter. "You don't say no to an opportunity to work with Jesse Lee Abel."

Snagging the stoic Jesse Lee had been Teddy's *coup de gras* for the gym. Not only did he attract the top indie talent, but they also had a sudden influx of gym members that were mostly fanboys hoping to catch a glimpse of the champion while they ran on the treadmill. Jesse was super professional but also a total rock; she could never tell if he actually liked the attention or just tolerated them all. That went double for people. The only person who ever got more than a cursory nod was Harper.

Raleigh laid a hand on his chest, running her palm over his pectorals. His chest was almost bigger than her tits and that made her just the teeniest bit salty. His skin was prickly; he'd need to shave or wax before the KAIGU show so that they could oil him up so he was nice and shiny for TV. Her hand skimmed a rosy nipple.

His chest rumbled with a sigh this time. "If you keep doing that, I'm probably going to get hard again." His voice was raspy with sleep.

Raleigh adjusted the blanket a little higher on his hips. "Rest. I'll make sure no one gets you."

"Promise?" She heard the smile in his voice.

She kissed his pec. "I promise."

Poor guy must have been dead on his feet because they were silent for about a minute before his breathing slowed and his body relaxed in the tell-tale signs of sleep.

Raleigh wished it were that easy for her, but her mind was still churning a million miles a minute. Leon's admonishment from earlier was like a splinter stuck in her hand: insidious, demanding her attention.

She wasn't the same kind of girl her mother was. She didn't want to trap August.

August was light and positivity and sweetness. She was so jaded about so many things. She didn't want him to catch her cynicism. She wanted him to kill his TV debut, get snatched up by one of the bigger promotions, leave this town and never look back.

Not even for her.

She was not good enough for August Callahan. She knew that in her bones. Leon more or less confirmed that and if he knew it, the whole town knew it.

She shouldn't want him as much as she did. She should be the bigger person, kick him out, let him go find someone as good as him. Someone who deserved him.

Waking up felt like dragging her consciousness through molasses. The room was still dark, so she'd probably only been asleep for a couple of hours. She was warm, overly so. Her legs were sticking out from under the blanket and there was something hard lodged between her butt cheeks.

Oh.

Oh.

She hadn't woken August up and kicked him out like she told herself she would. Oh, no. She'd let him spoon her in his sleep.

And it was fucking nice.

August's nose ran down her throat and she shivered. His lips came next. "Are you awake?" His voice was still raspy with sleep but that just made it hotter.

Raleigh adjusted her hips and he groaned, sucking on her throat. His free hand (not the one she was using as a pillow) spanned her soft belly, creeping slowly down.

Raleigh's body was at war with her head, and it was a fucking traitor. Her pussy practically quivered in anticipation as his fingers went down, down, down.

He brushed her swollen lips and her back arched. "August."

"God, I love hearing you say my name." His mouth locked onto her throat.

"I say your name all the time." She tried to joke, but the words came out high and breathy.

"Not like this."

He licked up her jaw, nipping at her earlobe. Raleigh moaned, pressing her ass back into the cradle of his thighs.

His fingers slipped between her folds and found her clit with a certainty he didn't have before. Her body throbbed, pressure building quickly in her hips, her thighs.

She grabbed his bicep for support. "I'm going to come again."

"I know."

She wanted to protest; it wasn't fair. They would be uneven.

Raleigh whined as the orgasm blasted through her middle with mind-numbing quickness.

August stroked her through it, peppering soft kisses down her throat and across her shoulder. His cock was hard as steel against her ass.

Her stomach was still fluttering as she sat up and stared down at him. She wished she was stronger.

"Are you sure you want it to be me?"

He smiled, a boozy, lopsided grin that almost stopped the heart in her chest. She wasn't going to survive August Callahan.

Raleigh sucked in a breath. "Okay. Do you have a condom?"

August's brow furrowed. She barked a short laugh. "Okay, second lesson of the night: always bring your own condom."

His eyes sparkled. "I think I've learned more than one lesson tonight, don't you?"

This time, it was Raleigh's turn to blush. The heat in her cheeks was unfamiliar. She was not a blusher. But there was something so dirty and intimate about the way *that* line just fell out of his mouth.

At a loss for a retort, Raleigh rolled over to her nightstand, grabbed a condom, and rolled back. She held it up for his inspection. If he'd never had sex, he probably needed a crash course on condom etiquette, right?

That's at least what she told herself as she started rambling. "They're all basically the same. Don't let anyone tell you differently. And don't pull it on too tight. You could tear one that way."

He listened with a slightly bemused expression on his face, which only seemed to make Raleigh ramble some more.

He grabbed her wrist to stop the spill of her words. "I think I've got it."

Chapter Eight
August

Raleigh was cute when she was flustered.

She was devastatingly pretty all the time but absolutely adorable when she was over-explaining condom usage to him with her ears pink.

August didn't mind, though, because he got to watch her mouth move.

He almost laughed at the shocked way her eyes widened when he grabbed her wrist and took the condom.

Her gaze flicked down his body, lingering at the apex of his thighs; she wet her bottom lip. August gripped his shaft and squeezed, the pressure making him exhale harshly. He was so hard, he felt like his balls were going to burst. Maybe his dick too. His whole body might just spontaneously combust.

Never in his wildest fantasies—and there were many—did he ever believe he could have Raleigh French. And she was basically naked beside him, oversized shirt slipping down her shoulder, nipples tenting the fabric, stormy eyes glazed and hungry. For him.

Her eyes tracked his movements as he tore the condom wrapper and slid the prophylactic down his shaft.

"Take your shirt off," he said. When did he become so demanding? Would she do it? Or be offended because he asked?

Her fingers gripped the hem, and it was halfway up her middle before she stopped. God, no. She couldn't stop now. He'd literally die.

"I'm not really looking for anything serious." The shirt was right under her tits. "I definitely want to fuck, but I'm not, like, a relationship girlie."

"Oh, yeah, right. Me neither."

Liar. You're a liar, August Callahan.

He wanted Raleigh. He'd wanted her since the first day he saw her flitting around behind the desk at the BPC. He may have even wanted her since he watched her strut across the graduation stage in her sparkly heels, even though he didn't know what that felt like at seventeen.

But he would never ask for more than she was willing to give. If Raleigh just wanted sex, that was fine with him. He would settle, he would live.

She stared at him for a few heartbeats; his dick was leaking into the condom. Her face was unreadable. Then she tugged the shirt the rest of the way off and tossed it. Tiny goose bumps covered her exposed skin.

"If you don't like anything, you have to tell me." Her usually airy voice was so serious.

He choked on a laugh. "I doubt I'll dislike anything you do to me."

Her lips tipped in a wry grin, like she was thinking of everything she could possibly do. He couldn't wait. August wanted it all.

She ran her hand over his chest, plucking at his nipples. August's stomach spasmed.

He huffed. "Will you just deflower me already? I'm dying." It was a whine. He was whining, almost begging. He'd beg if that's what she wanted.

Raleigh chuckled under her breath before giving one of his nipples a hard pinch that made his dick twitch.

She braced herself on his abs, sliding one of her legs over his hip. She gripped his dick and lined it up at her wet entrance. Oh, God, it was finally, really, happening.

August's lungs burned with his heaving breaths. His eyes were glued on her pussy, riveted to the spot where the tip of his cock split her pink lips.

She sunk down, excruciatingly slow, exercising an impressive display of thigh strength. She was braced on his chest, long nails pricking his skin, dark hair spilling over a rounded shoulder.

August couldn't think. All reasonable thought had been wiped from his brain by the slide of her pussy down his cock. He needed his thoughts, though. He needed to concentrate on not coming too fast. That would make it bad for her, right?

She seated herself fully on his cock, letting out the most exquisite sound. "Oh, fuck, you feel so good."

"Really?" August's voice was strained, strangled.

The sound she made lived somewhere between a moan and a laugh. "Really, baby boy."

Her hips started moving and August was lost. Was he supposed to be doing anything? Did he just get to watch her tits bounce? What was he supposed to do with his hands?

"Here." She gazed down at him with a soft expression, eyes crinkled in the corner with amusement. "Give me your hands."

They intertwined their fingers, and Raleigh used the support as leverage as she rocked her hips against him. August was mesmerized. He couldn't decide where to leave his eyes: the sway of her breasts, the way her stomach rolled, the muscles flexing in her thighs. She was *everything*. Her pussy was hot and tight and transcendent. He had never felt anything as good before her, and would never feel anything as good after her. His hips rocked up almost instinctually.

She moaned. "That's it, baby, move with me."

She pulled his hands to her stomach; he splayed his palms across her writhing damp flesh. She was panting now.

August slid his hands down, braced one on her hip and covered her mound with the other. He found her little clit with his thumb and rubbed in time with her hips.

"Fuck, yes, yes. Right there." She moaned, head tipping back.

August felt like he was going to explode. His chest was tight, his balls were tight, and the muscles that wrapped his spine were tight.

Raleigh's pace was almost frantic now; she was slamming herself down on his cock and his hand. She was demanding her pleasure from him.

He felt the moment it happened: the moment her pussy spasmed and clenched with her orgasm. It was enough for him. August's release pounded through him like a freight train; her pussy strangled his cock.

August hadn't lied to her. He'd done plenty of jacking off. But none of that came close to how it felt to come inside her.

He was wrung out, but Raleigh's hips moved more slowly, rocking them both through their orgasms. He felt his dick twitch a few more times.

He squeezed the round flesh at her hips.

Raleigh looked down at him, a soft, sensual look on her face, her mouth and strong jaw soft and relaxed. It was an expression he didn't think anyone else had ever seen. It was special, something just for him.

It didn't last long. Her lips twitched and it was like she put her mask back on. She patted his chest.

"You're a fast learner."

She slid off his hips, but instead of settling beside him again—which would have been August's preference—her delicate feet hit the carpet and she headed towards the en suite.

"I had a good teacher," he replied, just to match her tone.

He heard the shower come on. She was showering. August sat up and pulled the condom off, wrapping it up. He remembered seeing a small trash can in her kitchen. He got up, threw the condom away, and came back to the bedroom and she still hadn't emerged from the bathroom.

He got dressed.

Did she want him to leave? Was that supposed to be the order of things?

His T-shirt was still damp, and he still slightly smelled like fried chicken and dirty dishes. He also needed a shower.

He was spiraling.

He thought—there was a moment, he *swore* there was a moment—where he thought Raleigh might have felt the same way.

He had one foot in her room and one in the hallway when she emerged from the bathroom in a fluffy pink robe.

Her hair was up in a messy bun, tendrils wet around her face. "Are you leaving? You can shower."

Did she want him to leave? Or stay? Or shower then leave? His head was going to explode.

"I-I should get going. Early morning and late night again tomorrow."

She smiled, unbothered. She squirted some lotion on her hands as she passed him around the bed. "I imagine. Teddy wants you in fighting shape."

"Yeah."

It was lame. He was lame. He didn't have anything else to say.

You're a liar, August Callahan.

He had so much else he wanted to say, but wasn't brave enough to do it.

Chapter Nine
Raleigh

There was a sunflower on Raleigh's desk.

The day before it had been a carnation, and the day before, a rose. The same pale pink bow was tied around the stem.

Raleigh had no fucking clue how August was finding sunflowers in January.

She was a little late today—like she'd been the last few days—hoping the guys were already in the gym.

She told herself she wasn't actively avoiding August, not really. He was busy. He had rehearsals for KAIGU. They hadn't made any promises to each other. So why was guilt eating her up from the inside out?

She sat her purse on the front desk with a thump and scooped the sunflower into a shallow drawer with the wilted carnation and rose. That also made her feel guilty. But she couldn't take them home and she couldn't throw them away.

It was bad enough that she could still smell him on her pillows, even though she had washed all the bedding.

She was wiggling her mouse when Ben Ramirez sauntered through the front door, a gym bag slung over his shoulder and what looked like a blue shirt over his arm.

"Good morning, beautiful," he greeted. His attitude towards her never changed, so she assumed there were no hard feelings from New Year's. He'd been pretty drunk; maybe he forgot she'd gone home with him at all.

She raised her eyebrows as he dropped his bag and flung the T-shirt on her desk. "Good morning to you too, Benjamin."

He grinned at her. "Uh oh. My government name."

She tipped her chin. "What's this?"

He spread the shirt out, smoothing out wrinkles. August's face stared up at her from the fabric with the slogan, "Release the Goose" underneath in big, blocky letters.

"I'm still workshopping the tag line. Twenty bucks. We're all wearing them to the watch party at the bar. You can Venmo me."

"Goose? Who calls him Goose?"

"I'm pretty sure just me, but we're workshopping that too."

Raleigh felt her lips twitch. Goose was cute. She could imagine the way August's face would redden when or if he saw a bunch of people wearing his face. She pulled her phone out of her leggings.

"Fine. But you know merch is my job."

"It's not official merch." Ben showed her his QR code to scan and she sent him her size and money. "Appreciate your support."

He collected his stuff, about to finish his trek into the gym, but stopped and gave her a hard look.

"Be careful with my boy, understand?"

Her heart thumped. She glared right back at him. "What's that supposed to mean?"

"You know what it means. He's not like the rest of us."

Raleigh's first instinct was to deny that she even knew what Ben was talking about, but her throat was dry. And she knew he was right. August wasn't like them. He was better than them in so many ways.

She wouldn't snuff out his light, no matter how much it hurt them both in the process.

Since she couldn't manage a retort, she just nodded and Ben went on his way.

Her phone was buzzing. Teddy.

> Can you find our historical marketing budget or whatever?

> Harper is up to something

Raleigh shook her head and let out a little sigh. Teddy was resistant to moving his finance records entirely online; he still distrusted the internet for the most part. One of her big projects was moving all the BPC's records to bookkeeping software to make her and their accountant's lives easier. A lot of the records were still half and half, which was obnoxious. She and Harper were dragging Teddy into the twenty-first century, kicking and screaming, whether he liked it or not.

She finished stowing her stuff away and locked her computer before heading towards Teddy's office.

Raleigh had the physical records in the office meticulously organized, so it should be easy to lay hands on what Teddy wanted...unless he'd been in there moving things around again. He never did put things back where he found them.

She was elbow deep in a filing cabinet when she heard the door shut.

"Gimme a minute, Theodore. I'll find it."

He cleared his throat.

It wasn't Teddy Myles.

Raleigh turned around slowly, bumping the drawer closed with her hip.

August was leaning against the closed door. His short hair was damp, face flushed. He was shirtless, athletic shorts hanging low on his hips, exposing the deep cuts of his waist. There were red marks on his chest, most likely from taking practice chops in the ring.

Her pulse ratcheted, heart beating in her throat. She could do this. She knew she'd run into him again eventually.

"August, hey." She was proud that her voice came out relatively normal.

"Did I do something wrong?" August's emotions were written all over his face, in the lines of his body, the tremor in his question.

"No, of course not." It was on the tip of her tongue to ask why he would think that, but she already knew. Raleigh guessed she wasn't as slick as she thought she was.

"Are you avoiding me?"

"No, of course not."

She really needed to think of something else to say, but August had stepped closer and it was becoming hard for her to think.

"I liked the flowers," she said lamely, trying to find a safe place for her gaze.

His big hand closed over her elbow. She was wearing a long-sleeved athletic shirt but the fabric was thin and the heat of his palm sank into her skin.

He squeezed gently. "You can talk to me, you know, about what you're thinking."

But she couldn't. August was too good. If she told him she cared, that she *liked* him, that she liked him a little too much, he would take that seriously.

She'd be a distraction and she wouldn't do that to him.

She sucked in a breath. "Flowers are a relationship thing and we're not a relationship thing. Another lesson."

"I know. They're not a relationship thing. They're just a nice thing."

She wanted to tell him he shouldn't do nice things for her, but his hand had slid up her arm and across her shoulder. He brushed her jaw. Outlined her lips with the tip of his finger. When did he get so bold?

"I want to kiss you."

Her mouth twitched. August lost his virginity and got bossy.

"Here?" Her throat was dry.

"Yes."

She had to admit the danger of getting caught sent a little zip up her spine.

August stepped closer; they were chest to chest now, but he didn't stop. He backed her right into the wall, his knee nudging between her thighs. Raleigh's breath hitched. Her fingers brushed his abs and the skin jumped under her touch.

"Someone could see us." It was a weak argument and her roaming hands confirmed that.

"Is that a problem for you?"

His mouth hovered right above hers, so close she felt his breath. It *should* be a problem for her. It was very unprofessional of her to be making out in her boss's office, but her body didn't seem to care. Desire clenched her belly.

"How fast—" But her words were cut off by August's mouth.

The kiss was hot and hungry and claiming. She moaned into his mouth and sagged against him, but he held her pinned to the wall with his body. She ground her needy pussy against his hard thigh, whimpering as her body screamed for more.

August's hands pinned her wrists, his mouth kissing a sloppy line across her jaw and down her throat while she writhed against him.

"August, I need, I need..."

She wasn't even sure what she wanted to ask for. She was so empty and wanted him to fill her up and never stop. But she was greedy and the more he touched her the more she would want.

His hard cock pressed against her stomach.

Dangerous, this was so dangerous. But any sense of self-preservation was slowly eroded away by August's frantic hands. They were under her shirt, gripped roughly at her breast, pushed at the waistband of her leggings. The fabric got stuck on her hips, but she helped him roll it down her thighs. Her panties were next and then his palm was on her pussy.

He groaned, pressing his forehead to hers. "You're so hot here." His fingers pressed through her lips before finding her clit. "So wet." There was awe laced in his raspy tone.

"I need you to fuck me," she whined.

He chuckled. "Later. Promise me I'll see you later."

"Okay, fine, yes."

She moaned as he sunk two fingers inside her and rolled her hips against his hand. Raleigh dug her nails into his bicep and used her other hand to free his dick from his shorts.

August hissed, cock throbbing in her palm. He sunk his fingers deeper inside her, if that was even possible, setting a frantic pace. Raleigh matched him. It was hard and rough. August's whole body shuddered and she felt his hot release spray across her stomach. Raleigh came next, pussy sucking at his fingers.

They were both breathing rapidly; Raleigh felt stuck to the wall.

August kissed her forehead, a small smile playing around the corners of his mouth. He straightened his shorts, then grabbed the edge of one leg and wiped the cum off her stomach.

"I have a spare."

Raleigh straightened her own clothes, wishing she had brought fresh underwear. They'd be damp for the rest of the day. She'd think of him every time the fabric clung to her skin or her pussy throbbed.

She blew out a breath. August was looking shy again, his eyes flicking around her body like he wasn't quite sure what to do with her now.

She wanted to apologize. For avoiding him. For not saying anything about the flowers. For basically, for all intents and purposes, kicking him out of her condo after they'd had sex. She should have asked him explicitly to stay.

She grabbed his chin and pulled him down for a quick kiss. "Come over after your shift, okay? I'll stay up late."

He grinned at that, cheeks only slightly red as he left the office.

She waited for a beat. They shouldn't exit at the same time because that would probably look suspicious.

She should have apologized and left it at that.

Instead, she was just digging herself a deeper grave.

Raleigh was a shit cook.

It wasn't on the list of her mom's priorities growing up. She'd survived mostly on kid's frozen dinners with the brownies that turned into molten lava in the microwave and then were hard as rocks exactly one second later.

Still, she tried.

She thought it would be nice if August could have a hot meal after working basically two jobs today. He probably wouldn't be impressed because he probably knew how to cook because he was fucking perfect.

She only knew like two recipes from memory, and only had the ingredients for one. Tuna casserole. She just needed peas, tuna, cream of mushroom soup, and elbow noodles.

She was turning the stove down for the final congealing when she heard a soft tap on the patio door.

She knew it was August based on the unobtrusiveness of the knock.

He was standing on the patio in a hoodie with wet hair and a plastic bag, slightly out of breath.

"Did you run here?"

When he passed her, she noted that he smelled like spicy cologne and not fried chicken tonight.

"I went home and showered really quick, then came right over. I didn't want to be late. Or for your food to get cold." He held up the bag.

The night was looking up already. "You brought me food?"

He inhaled through his nose to regulate his breathing. "Yeah. Spinach and artichoke dip from the bar." He frowned as he set the bag on her island. "Might be cold anyway. Sorry."

He pulled out two to-go containers, one full of chips and another of spinach dip.

"Spinach dip is my favorite."

"Yeah, I know."

Raleigh's heart flopped. "How do you know?"

He blushed. "You always order it."

Raleigh sidled up next to him, their hips and shoulders brushing. His body heat practically engulfed her—it was comfortable and familiar. He opened up the to-go containers, and she couldn't help but watch his large hands.

She grabbed a chip, dipping it into the dip to break up the melted cheese on top, before loading it up and stuffing it in her mouth.

August smiled broadly, obviously pleased.

Raleigh managed to swallow before she said, "I made you dinner."

He glanced at her one lone, sad pot on the stove. "You did?"

She nodded, grabbing another chip.

August made a little humming sound in the back of his throat. His hands spanned her waist, moving her to stand more central in front of her chips and dip, which she did not mind at all.

He rubbed at her hips, over her ass. "I'm not hungry for food right now."

Raleigh's stomach swooped. She paused with a chip halfway to her mouth. "No?"

"Nope."

His fingers hooked her waistband and tugged her sweats down as he knelt on the floor behind her.

She heard his sharp inhale.

"You're not wearing anything else."

"Nope." She loaded up her chip.

August ran his hands up and down her thighs. His breath skimmed hotly across the base of her spine, an accompanying heat clenching in her lower belly. He pushed her thighs apart and Raleigh adjusted her stance, bracing one hand on the counter.

He ran a finger across the seam of her pussy. She quivered and he just hummed softly, fingers digging into the meat of her thighs as he spread her farther.

He started rubbing but his fingers barely brushed her clit. She wriggled, stomach digging into the counter, a hard line of frustration between her brows.

"August," she breathed.

He nipped at her thighs. "How's the dip?"

The dip had been momentarily forgotten.

The pressure of his fingers increased, and she let out a small gasp.

"Take a bite."

She did, shoving the whole chip in her mouth as one of his thick fingers sunk inside. She couldn't swallow fast enough.

A deep moan left her throat, eyelashes fluttering, pussy clenching around him. It was good, but not enough. She pressed down, trying to encourage his fingers towards her clit.

She felt his lips against the skin of her ass as he kissed and nipped, fingers kneading her flesh.

He withdrew his finger, spreading her own arousal across her lips and clit. The sudden pressure made her knees shake and she sighed in relief and desperation.

August finally brought his other hand to the task of finger fucking her. Two fingers rubbed her clit, the firm pressure making her hips buck, while he sank two fingers deep inside, crooking and curling them as she moaned desperately above him.

She was soaking his hands; the slippery, sucking sounds coming from her pussy filling the room.

He withdrew his fingers from inside her and she whined with frustration.

But then she felt him spreading her cheeks. No...he wasn't about to do what she thought he was about to do...was he?

Raleigh didn't have much time to think about it because then his nose was between her cheeks and his tongue was in her hole.

"Ohmyfuckinggod." She moaned, hands hanging onto the edge of the counter, practically sitting on his face.

She closed her eyes and pressed her sticky forehead against the Formica as the orgasm coiled tight in her belly. She was going to come with his fingers on her clit and his tongue in her ass.

A couple harder, determined thrusts of his tongue and she was done; the orgasm crashed over her. Her breath was a ragged keening and one of her hands slipped, knocking the container of chips into the sink with a clatter.

Her whole body quivered as he removed his hands and pulled up her sweats. He cupped her breasts as he reappeared over her shoulder; they were heavy and aching for a rougher touch.

"My chips," Raleigh said plaintively.

August chuckled. "I'll fix them."

He went to the sink and scooped up her chips like he didn't just have his face in her ass.

Raleigh's breathing was so ragged, she might pass out. "I did *not* teach you that."

His cheeks were slightly flushed, but his smile was pleased. "Seemed like a good idea."

Raleigh groaned; her knees felt like jelly.

What was she supposed to do with this man who stood in her kitchen like he belonged there, fixing her chips, after blowing her mind? A man who thought to bring over her favorite appetizer because he just happened to notice it was her favorite?

So, they ate her tuna casserole. Which was actually pretty good and not the worst struggle meal she knew how to make. Manwich sauce and spaghetti noodles took the top spot.

They had sex. Quickly, and then more slowly, which only served to confuse Raleigh further. Her head was muddied with orgasms and kindness.

After the sex, Raleigh stole August's hoodie and they played UNO on top of her bed. Raleigh crushed him, but August didn't seem to mind.

His gaze roamed around her room. "Can I ask you a question?"

Raleigh's stomach flipped. She shuffled her cards anxiously. "Sure."

"Why don't you have any stuff?"

Raleigh refused to feel embarrassed, even though she knew that wasn't the point of August's question. He had asked her something similar the first time he'd seen her place, and she'd given him a dismissive answer.

He appeared genuinely curious, waiting for her answer even though it was his turn.

"Well, I've only been here six months." She'd lucked into the condo. She was subleasing the place from an older couple who moved to Florida and weren't quite ready to sell yet. She was hoping they liked her enough to offer the place to her first and not put it on the market.

"You don't have any boxes, though."

Ah, he was too observant. Mostly everything she owned fit into her bedroom. Raleigh chewed her bottom lip. She was supposed to be distancing herself from August, not opening up her chest and letting him see her squishy innards. That was relationship shit.

"My mom was...kind of a hoarder, I guess? Not like, as bad as the show, but there was always so much random shit around. Piles of newspapers, DVDs, decorative watering cans. It was really weird. And our place was too small for all of it."

She knew why her mom did it. She was always trying to fill up the emptiness inside her with stuff they couldn't afford. Raleigh's attention was on her cards, but she couldn't really see them anymore.

She could feel August's eyes on her.

She shrugged, like it was no big deal. "It's just easier to have nothing."

"You don't have nothing. You have –" he cut himself off like he suddenly forgot what he was going to say. He took a breath. He wasn't looking directly at her anymore; they were both staring at their cards like Uno held the answers to all their problems.

He played a blue four, which matched neither the color nor the number that was currently face up on the pile.

"You could have me, if you wanted."

Raleigh played a red four. She couldn't want him because she wouldn't make him choose her when it was his time to leave this fucking two-stoplight town.

So, she said nothing and August took his turn.

Because she didn't have anything to say that wouldn't break her heart or flay her open.

Chapter Ten
August

There was nothing quite as exhilarating as the roar of a crowd. Their boos and cheers rippled through the arena like a wave, ebbing and flowing, shooting adrenaline through his body.

It always felt like this. Like home, like where he belonged. Everything else always faded away under the lights: his anxiety, his social awkwardness. He was not that person when he was in the ring. The only thing that mattered was the story, the press of the apron under his feet, the coarse rope under his palms.

The crowd loved Joel and by extension, August, because they were currently on the same team.

August leaned over the rope with his arm outstretched, urging Joel to make the tag.

The other tag team got to cheat—the best part of being the bad guys. They entered and exited the ring without an official tag, earning the ire of the audience. They took turns whaling on Joel while the crowd chanted their disapproval.

August stretched as far as he could go, body practically dangling off the top rope.

In a dramatic break from the other team, Joel lunged towards August, their palms smacking together.

Joel sagged against the turnbuckles as August leapt over the top rope. The other team made a big show of scrambling back as August crashed into the center of the ring.

August didn't get to make the pin this time—that was reserved for the main roster. But Joel pulled him into the ring and raised their fists in victory while the defeated team slunk off back up the entrance ramp.

It was hard to see the cameras with the overhead lighting, but August knew they were panning around the ring.

Joel gripped him in a sweaty side hug. "Good job, rook. Let's go. Commercial break."

They didn't have any more story after their match, so the cameras would go find something more interesting, a promo or some kind of out-of-ring conflict.

They walked back up the entrance ramp; Joel took his time, shaking hands with the audience lined up behind the gates, so August did the same until they were backstage again.

Backstage was crawling with producers and writers and sound guys, who all smacked him on the back and shoulders, congratulating him on the debut.

"Killer show, man."

"Super clean."

"Smooth as butter, baby."

A producer, one of the guys he recognized from his contract meeting, patted him on the back. "You feel up to talking to some media?"

August was basking in the post-performance afterglow, but the producer's question sent a little chill down his back. He wasn't a media guy. Yes, he was popular on social media, but he didn't do any actual *talking*. Just lifting and flexing.

"Oh, uh."

"Nothing scripted, just some questions about how you're feeling about your big debut. It'll be easy."

Could he even say no? He couldn't remember what exactly his contract said about media appearances. He was sure there was something. It was part of the gig. But what about spontaneous interviews?

The producer chuckled. "Don't look so concerned. A couple minutes is all. Just be yourself."

August nodded, and the producer steered him towards an area that looked like it was set up especially for media appearances. There were large banners with KAIGU's logo, some lights and tripods and reflectors. There were several cameramen already ready, and August recognized one of KAIGU's backstage correspondents holding the mic.

"He's all yours, Kiley." The producer gave August a little shove.

Kiley smiled. She was dressed super casually in jeans, boots, a nice blouse, and a cropped leather jacket. She gestured to a spot on the floor. "Right here."

August finally noticed the little red X created on the floor with tape. Must be the spot. His legs felt like lead. He would be sweating bullets if he wasn't already covered in sweat.

"Don't be nervous." She gave him another encouraging smile.

"Do I look nervous?" His voice felt raw.

"A little. But you don't have anything to be worried about. All easy questions, nothing out of left field. You go by August, right?"

He nodded. He could do this. He'd have to do this, if he wanted to become a professional. Media was part of the gig.

"Take a breath."

August did what Kiley said and inhaled and shook out his arms. He wasn't really sure what to do with his hands so he propped them on his hips. He felt stupid, but he'd seen plenty of other wrestlers do the same in interviews.

"Ready?"

August's breath puffed out but he nodded again.

Kiley did a couple of weird hand gestures to the cameramen and then she took up her own pose, stepping closer to August.

"And here we have August Callahan who made his KAIGU debut tonight. August comes to us from Cedar Creek, Kentucky. Is that right?"

"Uh, that's right."

"You currently train under heavyweight champion, Jesse Lee Abel, right? How does it feel to be under the wing of such a legend?"

Some of the tension eased from August's shoulders. She was throwing him soft ball questions. It was easy enough to talk about his hometown and his training under Jesse.

He was a hard-ass.

That made Kiley laugh and August finally cracked a smile of his own.

"You and Jesse share Cedar Creek as a hometown." She squeezed his bicep playfully. "They sure grow 'em big down there."

August's face flushed but Kiley was still laughing.

"So, do you think this will be a big break for you, August?"

"I hope so. I'm very thankful to KAIGU for giving me this opportunity. Wrestling has been my life for so long. I've never...uh, I've wanted this forever."

He'd almost told her that he'd never wanted anything else in his life as much as he wanted to make it in professional wrestling. But as soon as the thought crossed his mind, he knew it wasn't true. At least, it wasn't true anymore.

There was something...someone...he wanted more.

Kiley was talking and smiling at the cameras, but August couldn't really hear what she was saying anymore. There was a wild sort of roaring in his temples. It felt odd to finally admit to himself that he wanted Raleigh.

Kiley tipped the mic back towards him. "Before we go, is there anyone at home you want to give a special shout-out to?"

August knew it was a throwaway question. He'd heard it asked to a hundred wrestlers during post-match interviews. They expected it to be an easy question. Family. Coaches.

The roaring increased.

He was about to do something stupid.

Maybe even torch his career.

Guess he'd have to wait and find out.

He grabbed the mic, tipping it closer to his mouth. He found one of the cameras and stared into the black lens like it was her face, her stormy eyes, her pouty lips.

She was going to be so pissed at him.

"Yeah," he said. "Raleigh French. She thinks she doesn't want to be my girlfriend, but I think she's wrong. And I want the whole world to know I don't want anyone but her."

Chapter Eleven
Raleigh

Raleigh had never seen the bar so busy.

The parking lot was completely full; cars lined Pond Run Road and she was pretty sure filled the driveways of some of the adjacent houses.

Almost every person was wearing Ben's blue shirt. Everywhere she looked, August's screen-printed face stared back.

It was good that basically the whole town showed up for him. They all wanted him to get out too.

She squeezed into the bar until she saw Harper's orange head at a table with Ben and some other guys from the gym.

Harper waved enthusiastically.

Raleigh shoved her way through the crowd.

"Finally." Harper exhaled a relieved breath. "I almost had to fight an old lady for your chair."

Ben looked over his shoulder and nodded. "That's true."

Raleigh slid into the chair; there was barely enough room for her to pull it out properly. The top of the table was covered with appetizers and glasses, with pitchers of beer and margaritas. She poured herself a glass of beer and took a sip. It was lukewarm. She grimaced.

Harper raised one of her immaculate brows. "That's what you get for being late."

Raleigh had almost not shown up at all. But she felt that would raise more questions than she was ready to answer. Her absence would have been too noticeable. She took a bigger sip of the beer and focused her attention on the large screen TV over the bar.

She tried to ignore the fact that Harper was burning a hole in the side of her head with her suspicious eyes.

"What?"

"You've been weird lately."

"Weird how?"

Harper shook her head, her long nails drilling on the tabletop. Her gaze flicked to Ben, who'd gotten up to get another pitcher of beer, but was currently shamelessly flirting with a man in tight dark wash jeans and a cowboy hat who was blushing.

"You never told me how New Year's went."

"Oh, I didn't?" Raleigh's voice jumped a guilty octave.

Harper made a sound, pursing her lips and waiting. They hadn't known each other very long, but she really liked Harper. There wasn't much she hadn't told Harper, especially after one drunken night where they spilled all their darkest secrets to each other. Well, Harper's hadn't been especially dark. Thanks to some gossipy wrestling blogs, everyone knew most of her sordid family drama.

"Nothing happened. Ben and I are fine."

"Didn't meet anyone else over there, did you?"

Did everyone know August and Ben were roommates except her?

What was she supposed to say? That she had met someone. August was cute and hot and unintentionally funny and kissed her like he needed her to live? That she had broken all her rules and her heart ached?

That she might—*might*—love him but she wasn't going to say that out loud? No, she wouldn't say that to anyone, not even August. She'd take that confession to her grave as long as it meant August got out.

"Well, if you won't tell me your secrets, I'll tell you mine." It was an abrupt change in topic, but Raleigh wasn't going to complain.

Harper leaned over the table conspiratorially. "They're gonna induct Jesse into the Hall of Fame. In April."

"What?" Raleigh squawked. "No way."

Harper shushed her. "Keep your voice down. They haven't released the names for this year's class yet. No one else knows, except me and Dad and now you."

Teddy's sudden interest in their marketing budget now made sense. "Your dad is plotting something, isn't he?"

Harper slouched back in her seat and rolled her eyes fondly. "First August's debut and now this. The man might die from happiness...and sponsorship opportunities."

They both laughed.

"More work for me," Raleigh said.

Harper tipped her glass of margarita. "You better ask for a raise."

They clinked glasses. "Good call."

Ben slid back into his seat, some of his curls mussed over his forehead.

"Where've you been?" Harper asked. She jabbed a pointy-nailed finger accusingly at him. "And you didn't bring refills."

Ben had come back to the table empty-handed. He grinned at Harper over his shoulder before turning his chair around so he could sit on it backwards.

"Hush. Our boy is almost on."

"Making his way to the ring, in his very first KAIGU debut, from Cedar Creek, Kentucky, weighing in at two hundred and sixty pounds...August Callahan!"

August stepped out from behind the entrance curtain and the whole bar erupted into cheers and hoots and hollers.

Ben was practically bouncing in his seat like a little kid. "He looks good, doesn't he?"

He did, there was no denying that. His chest was positively ripped and his shiny purple leggings clung to his thighs like a second skin. Unlike literally every other time she saw him, there was no red staining his cheeks.

He raised both arms and waved, a shy but earnest grin stretching his mouth. They would love him.

"And joining him in the ring, current KAIGU All-Star Champion, Joel Nelson."

August was thicker than Joel, who had a thin and wiry build, but they were about the same height. His build was perfect for throwing and leaping and his signature move was an arm twist ropewalk chop off the top rope.

Harper grabbed Raleigh's arm and shook it with excitement. "Here we go!"

Her excitement was infectious. It was hard to be moody and put out—even if that was her own fault—when almost the whole damn town gathered to watch the guy you were hooking up with wrestle on TV.

She cheered and booed with the rest of them. August took a particularly hard elbow chop, which had Ben hurling obscenities at the TV.

"I think there are kids here, dude," Raleigh said.

"I don't give a fuck," he retorted, not even bothering to turn his head around.

Raleigh couldn't blame him. It was an exciting match. The other team was on top for most of the match, cheating mostly, and hamming it up for the cameras. Joel made a dramatic tag, let August come in and wipe the floor with the bad guys for a while, before they tagged out again and Joel made the final pin.

Harper was squealing beside her, even though she most likely knew the outcome of the match.

Ben had flipped his chair over when he stood and was pointing at the TV. "That's my boy!"

August was sweaty and panting but had the biggest, goofiest smile on his face. Almost like he was punch drunk. He was so happy. He was the brightest thing in the entire arena.

A strange sort of new emptiness filled her. She knew she'd done the right thing. August was too sweet to reject her, so she had to do it for him before they got any more entangled than they already were.

She was right.

She'd done the *right* thing.

It didn't matter that she felt like shit about it. She would handle it so August didn't have to.

Raleigh stood, chugging the rest of her glass of warm beer, which was even worse than when she'd first sat down.

Harper looked startled. "Where are you going? They haven't done any post-match interviews yet."

"I've got work to do." The lamest excuse.

Harper thought so too because her eyes narrowed, liner sharp enough to cut. "It's a Saturday night. You don't have any work to do."

Raleigh puffed out a breath. "Just let me leave."

Her chest was tight, eyes prickling. If she was going to cry, she wanted to do it alone, in her car or her empty bed.

Harper stood, her face creasing with worry and grabbed Raleigh's hand. "Hey, are you okay? What's going on?"

Raleigh shook her head. No. No, she was not okay. But she would *be* okay, and that's what mattered. She was always okay, no matter what shit life threw her way.

"Can I tell you later?" Her voice was strained, and she'd be surprised if Harper heard her over the noise in the bar.

But she nodded. "Yeah, sure."

Raleigh took a step away from Harper, not enough to break their hand hold, but then she froze because she heard August's voice. He was doing a backstage interview, and she was so bound and determined to be a masochist that she turned to watch. She'd watch the interview and then go. Maybe get some ice cream and tequila on her way home to nurse her shredded heart.

Kiley Marsh was a regular commentator for KAIGU and also had her own wrestling podcast, *The Highspot*. She was just asking really basic questions, but August still looked nervous as fuck. It was a stark contrast to his demeanor walking down the entrance ramp.

She hoped Kiley had enough experience and wherewithal to tell how uncomfortable he was.

And then she asked, "Before we go, is there anyone at home you want to give a special shout-out to?"

His whole body morphed, like he was becoming a different person, or shedding a skin. His shoulders dropped, his chin tilting up. He made direct eye contact with the camera and Raleigh felt like he was looking right at her...even though she knew that wasn't possible.

"Yeah," he said. "Raleigh French. She thinks she doesn't want to be my girlfriend, but I think she's wrong. And I want the whole world to know I don't want anyone but her."

Her whole world stopped.

The noise in the bar was a dull roar in her ears.

She could feel Harper shaking her whole damn arm but couldn't hear a word she said.

Raleigh's heart may have stopped beating.

August knew she'd be watching. He knew the whole town would be watching.

She couldn't slink away and hide anymore. No. Because now *everyone* knew. Everyone and their cousins and siblings and step-kids and whatnot.

There were a pair of big tits pressed into her side.

Harper was hugging her.

Like this was *good*.

Instead of *devastating*.

"I...I can't believe he said that." Raleigh finally found her voice.

Harper was gushing. "It's so romantic. Like something right out of a movie."

No. No, didn't she see how bad this was? She hadn't been in the meeting with the KAIGU reps. The producers. They had specifically asked if August was in a relationship. They had asked him to keep things the way they were, not blow up his whole fucking fledging career on regional TV.

If he violated his contract, he was done. They wouldn't agree to let him finish the storyline, would most likely never contract him again, probably blacklist him, and make him return most, if not all, of the money.

"I have to go."

"Where are you going?"

Harper was hot on her heels as she practically sprinted out the door.

"I have to go to the office." Raleigh's purse swung wildly as she hunted down her car keys.

Harper was at her passenger side door, her hand obstinately on the door handle. "I'm coming with you."

"You are not."

"I am too. If you're having some kind of meltdown, I feel like it's only my duty as your best friend to be involved."

"You're not my best friend," Raleigh grumbled, getting into the car and stabbing her key in the ignition.

Nothing stopped Harper, though. Not even Raleigh being a bitch. She hopped right in and buckled up.

"I'm almost one hundred percent sure I'm your only friend, so..."

So. She was unfortunately probably correct.

Raleigh could feel Harper staring at her, but she refused to look over. She knew Harper was dying to probe, but she was silent in the car.

She didn't say anything when Raleigh disabled the alarm, or unlocked the front doors of the BPC, or opened the door to Teddy's office.

Raleigh had a copy of August's contract spread out on the desk in front of her when Harper cleared her throat.

She wasn't subtle at all.

"Sooooo. Are you going to tell me what's going on now?"

Her eyes skimmed the paragraphs. It was a lot of legalese, a lot of it pretty standard for temporary contracts. She couldn't find anything that actually specified August had to maintain any kind of relationship status. It must have just been a throwaway comment from the producer. Nothing written in stone.

She would have already known that if she hadn't been so busy watching August during the contract meeting.

She let out a breath, the knot in her chest loosening, like she hadn't taken a full breath since the end of August's interview. So, it wasn't so bad. She could fix this.

She finally looked up.

Harper was standing across from her, arms crossed and her hip cocked like some kind of inked-up preschool teacher.

Raleigh's fingers fluttered over the pages of the contract. She didn't have any other excuses that could explain the last half hour.

"I just needed to check August's contract." She flipped the folder closed, like that closed the case.

"Why?"

Raleigh played with the edge of the folder, not meeting Harper's stern look. "I needed to make sure there weren't any...relationship clauses."

"Because of what he said?"

Raleigh nodded.

"Okay, so that explains why we're here. It doesn't explain why you looked like somebody died. I don't think I've ever seen someone look so devastated to find out a hot guy wants to date them."

Raleigh let out a breath, her head falling back. "You don't understand." She might as well tell Harper how she felt since it seemed like the girl wasn't going to let it go. Raleigh straightened. "I'm not good enough for him."

Harper made a dismissive, scoffing noise. "That's such bullshit."

"It's not." She spread her hands. "I'm nobody. Just some hick girl from the middle of nowhere. August is better than that. He's going to go places."

"And he can't go places if he has a girlfriend?"

"I don't want him to think there's something left for him in this town."

"Okay, first off..." Harper held up her fingers like she was going to start counting down her points. "You're smart and pretty and you have a great ass. You're probably *too* good for him, if I'm being totally honest. A little mean, sometimes, but we all have our flaws. And, as someone who spent most of her life running from this town, it's really not that bad, if you rule out the rednecks and the bigots." She offered a small smile.

"That's, like, fifty percent of the population."

"Yeah, but most of them are really old and are gonna be dead soon. So, we really need you."

Raleigh snort-laughed and then sniffed. Tears had managed to free themselves from her eyes and trickled down her cheeks. This is what happened when people were nice to her.

She choked on a sob, biting down on her bottom lip.

"Oh, honey."

Harper rounded the desk and wrapped Raleigh up in her shorter arms, shoving her face right into her tits, which honestly wasn't a bad place to be if she was losing her shit.

Raleigh let the tears come for a minute, while Harper rubbed circles between her shoulder blades.

She pushed away. "Okay. I'm done, I'm done." She swiped at her eyes and runny nose.

Harper grabbed a tissue from the box on Teddy's desk and handed it to her. Raleigh cleaned her face up the best she could.

"So, I think it's pretty obvious we've discovered that you do, in fact, have feelings."

Raleigh shot her a glare, which was probably less impressive than normal considering her puffy eyes.

Harper shrugged. "Some of us weren't sure. What's your plan now? You're gonna get your man, right?"

Raleigh felt something weird unfurl in her chest. Something she didn't feel very often. It might have been hope.

Chapter Twelve
August

August was in trouble.

But, like, not really.

Teddy was just blowing off some steam.

He did, unfortunately, feel like a kid who'd been called to the principal's office as he sat in a chair in front of Teddy's desk while Teddy ranted behind it.

August had barely made it to the gym Monday morning before Teddy'd found him and dragged him to the office. He hadn't even seen Raleigh yet...he was trying to give her some space. He had made his intentions clear, so it was her turn now. The waiting was killing him. Making his skin itch. It was distracting, so much so that he barely heard what Teddy said but he was pretty sure it was something like "dumb fucking kids" and "I'm too old for this."

"Perry called me yesterday. On a Sunday! Do you know how bad it must be for those guys to call on the weekend?"

August frowned. "Who's Perry?"

Teddy sputtered. "Who-who's Perry? The fucking KAIGU producer."

Ah. August hadn't caught any of their names.

"They're upset with you."

"They said the interview was unscripted."

"It was."

"Can they do anything about it?"

Teddy sighed like he carried the whole entire wrestling world on his shoulders. "No, not right now. They may never book you again, you know. They don't like talent going rogue."

August sat with that. He knew that was the risk. He was (admittedly) relieved that he hadn't broken any of his contract terms, but as far as future gigs...

He waited for the panic to set in. The anxiety.

He heard Raleigh's voice in his head. He was the star, he was the talent, he had the half million followers.

August felt settled in his bones. He smiled. "How were their ratings?"

Teddy speared him with a glare. "Don't be getting sassy with me, boy."

August drummed his fingers on the armrests. "Harper said my interview is going viral."

Teddy's face purpled like a fresh bruise. He jabbed a finger at August. "I'm gonna spin this, ya hear? You just got lucky for pulling that little stunt."

"That's why you're the boss." August stood. "I'm late for training."

"Yeah, you better get out in that ring, you little shit." He was waving his cell phone at August's back as he shut the door so Teddy couldn't see him laughing.

He practically skipped back down the hallway, feeling lighter than he had in days. His career wasn't ruined. Raleigh knew how he felt. There was only one obstacle left.

He froze because Raleigh was standing at the front desk, staring at him, like she'd known where he was and was waiting for his dressing down to end.

She looked radiant in a pair of high-waisted powder blue leggings, matching blue Nike Dunks, and a cropped sweater that showed a sliver of skin on her sternum. The outfit was basically what she wore every day, but her hair was down in wavy dark curls and it looked like she had the big lashes on again. Her lips were a perfect, glossy pink and he just wanted to kiss her and never stop.

She blinked when she saw him, but composed herself quickly, drawing her shoulders back and propping a hand on one of her hips.

"Did he fire you?"

August grinned so wide it made his cheeks hurt. "Nope."

She snorted, gaze glancing down to the hand she had propped on the desk and back again. "You shouldn't have pulled a stunt like that."

He stepped to her until they were toe to toe and he could look down at her.

She glared up at him. "Don't loom over me like that, you troglodyte."

She shoved his chest, but he didn't move. She'd have to do better than that to push him away. Raleigh tried again, but this time, August caught her fingers up in his.

He pulled her hand up to his mouth and kissed the back of her knuckles. There was still fire in her eyes, but her lips had softened into a cute little pout.

He wanted to kiss her forever. He wanted her to glare at him forever.

He nipped at her skin and she sighed, big lashes fluttering like fans.

"You can't do this to me, August."

"Do what?"

"Be all romantic and sweet and make grand declarations like we're in some kind of rom-com." The corners of her mouth tipped down. "Please tell me you didn't ruin your career."

"Nope." He squeezed her fingers. "Tell me you don't want me."

"I can't."

Her voice was soft and breathy and a little broken, like it physically hurt her to admit her feelings for him.

"Then we should give the people what they want."

"And what's that?"

"A love story."

She snorted, but then a bit of horror crossed her face. "What do you mean, give the people what they want?"

"Oh." He flushed. "Harper said we're going viral."

"I can't believe you." She yanked her hand from his grip and swatted at him, but August wasn't letting her go so easily.

He snatched her waist and hoisted her up, plopping her down on the front desk with a squeal. He held her there with both hands on the swell of her ass.

"People are going to see."

But she wrapped her legs around his waist and her arms around his shoulders.

"Let them watch."

She rolled her eyes. "And here I thought you were so sweet and innocent."

He kissed her. He was done with her deflections and evasion. He kissed her hungrily, like he could pour all his heart into her mouth.

Raleigh moaned deep in her throat, her thighs squeezing him.

Breaking the kiss was one of the hardest things August had ever done, but she still hadn't answered him and he needed an answer.

"Say yes." His mouth ghosted her jaw.

She arched into him. "Yes to what?"

"I want you to be my girlfriend. A whole real relationship."

She averted her gaze, lashes fluttering, looking at his chin instead of his eyes. It was almost shy. "Okay."

"Okay, what?"

She pulled on the short hair on the back of his neck. "Okay, August Callahan, I'll be your girlfriend."

He grinned. "Promise?"

"Promise." She leaned in closer; he could smell her shampoo, the vanilla hints on her skin. "Kiss me again like that."

August did, capturing her mouth with his roughly, squeezing her ample ass and hips.

"Oh, for fuck's sake, I should fire you both."

They broke apart only to see Teddy in the lobby.

Raleigh let out a peal of laughter, and it was the most beautiful sound August had ever heard. It made her eyes sparkle.

She pushed August away and then slid off the desk like they hadn't just been caught making out. She flipped her hair.

"You could, but then you wouldn't have anyone to balance your books, find your records, create your merch, manage your sponsorships..." Her voice trailed off as she followed a grumbling Teddy into the gym, still listing off all her duties at his back.

August rubbed his lips; she'd left traces of her sticky lip gloss. He smiled as he headed to the locker room.

Jesse was probably under orders to punish him, but August didn't care.

It was going to be a good day.

Epilogue

Raleigh had been August "The Goose" Callahan's official girlfriend for a month. She hadn't had a *boyfriend* boyfriend since high school. It was kinda nice. Not that she would admit that to anyone, except maybe August.

Ben was also still trying to make "The Goose" happen, but it wasn't quite sticking, even though he insisted that geese were, objectively, actually terrifying.

It was Valentine's Day and August insisted they go out.

Raleigh adjusted the ties that were holding the bodice of her skin-tight red dress together. She always had to make the top smaller, even though the fabric was fighting for its life over her ass.

There was a knock on her patio door. August was early; she hadn't even finished putting her face on yet.

She stumbled to the door in her strappy black heels.

August had his arms full. She spied a heart-shaped box of candy under a bouquet of red roses and a white bear with a fuzzy red heart on the belly. Did he buy the whole store out?

He was in joggers, Vans, and a hoodie.

"What are you wearing?"

He peered around the bouquet. "What are *you* wearing?"

She spun around on her heel so he could get the full experience of the dress. "You said we were going out."

"Oh." His cheeks reddened. "I was thinking, uh, bowling. They're having a Valentine's Day special."

She stepped back so August could come in. "Well, you know I can't resist a special."

August shuffled adorably. "Are you sure? We can do something else. Whatever you want."

She took the bouquet to free up one of his hands. "I want to bowl. I just need a new outfit." She set the flowers on the countertop.

August followed her back to the bedroom, spilling the rest of his armful on the end of her bed. She noticed that there was a wrapped box among the loot.

She smiled. "All of this for me?"

He stepped closer, his cologne tickling her nose; she felt the tips of his fingers brush across her back, right over the line of her dress.

She shivered and let the warm, happy feelings consume her for a moment. It was still so early, and she was still waiting for the other shoe to drop. For August to finally wise up and realize he could do better.

He was making a run for the KAIGU tag team championship, after all. After crunching their numbers after August's debut and dramatic televised declaration, they'd already extended his contract.

But August was showing no indications of leaving. He was unflappable in the face of her general surliness. An extra toothbrush had magically found its way to the cup on her bathroom counter and his hoodies were in her laundry.

But he definitely wasn't moving in.

He just left stuff at her house. And slept over a lot.

They had gone to Macy's and she spent several hundred dollars on a new couch and almost passed out when the cashier swiped her credit card.

Then they went to the thrift store and found a cute, vintage coffee table that was still in good shape. She'd taken the woven throw blanket from her bed and put it across the back of the couch. The pink and navy looked cute together.

She had furniture. Almost like a real adult. And it felt good to have *things*.

One of her thin straps had fallen down. August's lips brushed across the curve of her shoulder.

"I've never gotten flowers for Valentine's Day before. Did you know that?" She'd never gotten anything for Valentine's Day before, but that made her sound sad, so she kept it to herself.

"Yeah."

He found the tiny zipper at the side of her dress and tugged it down. His large hands spanned her waist, one slipping down her stomach.

She felt his inhale. "Are you not wearing underwear?"

Raleigh laughed. "Yeah, that was supposed to be your gift."

She felt the teensiest bit guilty that she didn't get him a real gift, but they hadn't discussed gifts. And she waxed the majority of her body for him. She could send him the bill from the wax lady who shaped her bush into a heart for the occasion.

He sucked on her neck, palm brushing over said bush, fingers teasing her lips apart.

"I love my gift." His voice was quiet against her skin, but started a cacophony in her head. They had not said the L word to each other yet, and she was resisting. Her logical brain said it was much too soon, but she was having a hard time convincing her body and her heart that *this* didn't feel like love.

His hands on her body felt like stability.

She never had to ask for help; he was just there, like he couldn't resist. He carried furniture, installed curtain rods, smiled at her frilly pink curtains, brought her a keychain from a gas station on the way back from the KAIGU arena that said "Anne." It was her middle name because you could never find "Raleigh" on those keychains.

August *saw* her in a million tiny, tender, unexpected ways. He liked what he saw and never found her lacking or wanted her to be different.

His hot mouth trailed over her shoulder. "You should open your present now."

She eyed the rectangular box on the bed. It was wrapped in purple paper and had a big pink bow.

August pulled his hands from her dress—a shame—so she could grab the package, but not before he tugged the straps down her arms. The fabric pooled on her hips, but August worked it down her thighs as she ripped the cute paper off the present.

Raleigh's breath caught, thighs clenching. August was stroking her hips. She was naked, save her for a strapless long line lacy bra.

She'd unwrapped a beginner's strap-on kit. According to the box, the harness, dildo, and lube were included.

"You got me a strap-on?"

"Yes." His breath was hot on her neck.

"You've been googling things again, haven't you?"

His answer was the press of his tongue on her spine, the swell of his cock against her ass. Raleigh's center throbbed.

Raleigh opened the box. The harness was black and the dildo was hot pink. She bit her lip to keep from giggling.

She caressed the dildo in her hands. "You want me to fuck you?"

August whimpered, teeth scoring her shoulder. "Shit, yes."

"I thought we were going bowling?" Now she was just teasing him.

His fingers brushed her pussy again. "They're open until midnight."

Raleigh almost snorted. Yeah, like they were going to leave the bed once they got in it. She knew better.

"Lie down." Her voice was a touch breathy. She had never pegged anyone before, even though the idea always intrigued her. It would be a first time for both of them.

August stripped his clothes at the speed of light and jumped on the bed like someone told him he won the lottery. He was grinning, two blooms of color on his cheeks. He propped himself up on his elbows, thighs splayed, cock already mostly hard against his stomach.

Raleigh pulled on the harness, adjusting the straps against her thighs and waist until it felt comfortably snug against her pubic bone and mound.

The dildo clicked in easily to the O ring; it was thin and sleek.

Raleigh took a few practice thrusts, and the dildo wiggled in a way that made her laugh.

August groaned, falling back with a hand clapped over his eyes. "Stop. You're ruining the mood." But there was affection in his voice.

Raleigh placed both hands on her hips and thrust again. "What? I'm practicing." She let out a breath at the twinge in her abs. "That's kinda hard."

August snort-laughed, but then he rolled onto his hands and knees and arched his back and nothing was funny anymore. He was stunning.

August looked over his shoulder. "Still need to practice?"

Raleigh swallowed, throat dry. The muscles that corded his back rippled as his shoulders dipped towards the mattress.

She grabbed the small bottle of lube and got up on the bed behind him, running a palm over the smooth roundness of his ass. August shuddered.

Raleigh slicked the pad of her thumb and the head of the dildo. She didn't have any short fingernails. She felt nervous. And powerful. It was a heady mixture that had her almost lightheaded.

She gently spread his fat cheeks and pressed her thumb to his hole. August made a strained choking noise.

She applied the lube generously with her thumb before replacing it with the dildo.

"You have to let me know if anything doesn't feel right, okay?"

August huffed. “God, yes, okay.”

Raleigh couldn’t contain her grin. He was so desperate. So perfect and desperate. She used the head of the dildo to work him open and he heaved beneath her. Lube was dripping. Her pussy throbbed in time with August’s gasping breath.

She eased the dildo in deeper, inch by tiny inch, almost holding her breath as she met resistance and then slipped past it.

August moaned, the sound long and drawn out as he buried his face in the bed, his hips pushing back against hers.

“Careful, pretty boy,” she cooed, rubbing the small of his back. Raleigh kept stroking his skin as she tried little experimental thrusts, timing them to August’s whines.

It was a strange, unfamiliar sensation. Nothing was touching her clit, but the strap harness was rubbing against her thighs and labia, ratcheting up her own pleasure.

She moved her hands up to grip his hips for better leverage. August panted, the breath sawing in and out of his lungs.

More strange sensations. She couldn’t *actually* feel his body clenching around the dildo, but she could imagine it and that was almost just as good.

August moaned. He begged. He chanted nonsense words that she couldn’t hear because his forehead was pressed to the mattress. Could she make him come like this?

Just the thought clenched her stomach. The harness was going to be soaked.

Raleigh risked taking one hand off his hip so she could reach around and grasp his dick. He was hot and hard and her fingers were already so messy with the lube. It was a little awkward, trying to keep up both movements at the same time, but she didn't have to for long.

August came on a cry, his whole body shaking as hot cum coated her fist.

He collapsed on the bed, practically popping himself off the dildo with a wet sucking noise. She flopped beside him, dildo still swinging. She needed to catch her breath before undoing the harness.

August's face was sweaty and flushed and he beamed at her, that open, sweet smile that always tugged at her heart.

"I think I love you," he said.

Raleigh's heart stopped. "You can't say stuff like that after sex. It's the endorphins."

August wasn't fazed, though. "It's okay if you're not ready to say it, Raleigh. You don't have to right now. But I—"

"I love you," she blurted. "I mean, I love you, too." She meant it, because she *did* feel it. And she was so damn tired of not getting what she wanted. Of settling for nothing because that's all she expected.

August wasn't nothing. He was everything.

His eyes shimmered. "You're not just saying that because I let you peg me, right?"

Raleigh choked on her laugh and grabbed his face. "Well, that." She pressed a kiss to his forehead. "And the way your ass looks in a pair of leggings, obviously."

He fake growled and rolled on top of her, the dildo pressed between their stomachs. He stole her mouth, the kiss hungry and raw and honest.

"Good. Cause that's the only reason I love you too. The way your ass looks in leggings, prancing around the gym." His mouth quirked.

She laughed, cupping his face. "You promise?"

"Promise."

Afterword

Thank you for reading *Dark Match*! I hope you enjoyed Raleigh and August's story and are ready to prop up your feet and stay for a long time in Cedar Creek, Kentucky. A good time is guaranteed!

Reviews are one of the best ways to support an author, so I would love you forever if you left one (or even just some stars!) somewhere on the internet. Be sure you're following me for updates about the series. Who's next? You'll just have to wait and see!

Did you really, *really* enjoy this story and want to dive deeper into the Jessica-verse? I would be absolutely tickled if you joined me on Patreon! You can get free eBooks, sticker mailings, behind-the-scenes updates, bonus content, early access, art, and can start reading my unhinged paranormal romance serial, *Guilty As Sin*

About the Author

J.L. Minyard is the not-so-secret pen name of award-winning young adult author Jessica Minyard. Jessica is an author, poet, ISTJ, Sagittarius, and boy mom who lives and writes from the bluegrass.

Check out both her contemporary series:

Penn Warren University

Bluegrass Performance Center

For freebies, sneak peeks, and other updates, head to jessicaminyard.com to sign up for her newsletter or join her on Patreon.

Follow her on social media:

facebook.com/jessicaminyardbooks

instagram.com/callmeshashka

tiktok.com/@jessicawritesromance

amazon.com/stores/J.L.-Minyard/author/B0B7R171CP

MINYARD'S MINIONS

WANT MORE?

BECOME A MINION ON PATREON!

What is Patreon?

Patreon is a way for readers to directly support authors while getting access to special bonus goodies like early access to projects, exclusive content, and physical merch.

How can I get started on Patreon?

Create a free account and find me here:

https://www.patreon.com/minyardsminions

www.ingramcontent.com/pod-product-compliance
Lightning Source LLC
LaVergne TN
LVHW051004080826
845145LV00009B/2455

* 9 7 8 1 9 5 7 0 0 4 1 9 8 *